Lock Down Publications and Ca$h
Presents

I0637479

THE REAL BADDIES OF CHI-RAQ 2

SEASON 2

Written By
KING RIO

First Edition 2025

Printed in the United States of America

This is a work of fiction. Names, characters, places, and incidents either are products of the author's imagination or are used fictitiously. Any similarity to actual events or locales or persons, living or dead, is entirely coincidental.

Lock Down Publications
P.O. Box 944
Stockbridge, GA 30281
www.lockdownpublications.com

Like our page on Facebook: Lock Down Publications
www.facebook.com/lockdownpublications.ldp

Stay Connected with Us!

Text **LOCKDOWN** to 22828 to stay up-to-date with new releases, sneak peaks, contests and more...

Like our page on Facebook:
Lock Down Publications

Join Lock Down Publications/The New Era Reading Group

Visit our website:
www.lockdownpublications.com

Follow us on Instagram:
Lock Down Publications

Email Us: We want to hear from you!

The Real Baddies Of Chi-raq 2

I'd like to extend a huge thanks to every reader who's ridden with me thus far. When I first penned The Cocaine Princess series, I never thought that so many more novels would follow. If either of my books have entertained you throughout your days, evenings, or nights, I am deeply grateful. God willing, there will be plenty more to come.

In this sequel to *The Real Baddies*, I wrote with everything I had in me— mainly because some asshole threw away the book when I was just about finished and I had to start over from scratch, but also because certain characters and scenes required a great deal of thought before putting pen to paper

Well, I hope you all enjoy the read. God bless.

Undying Love, Rio

Follow me on social media:
Facebook: Author Rio
Author King Rio
Instagram: @authorrio5

Prologue
Little Duffle Bag Girls

"It's all there," the tall, broad-shouldered man said to Aqua as she sat forward on the threadbare gray sofa and ran another thick pile of twenty-dollar bills through the digital money counter. "I counted it twice myself and then sent it through my own money machine just to be sure. It's all there, lil lady. Five hundred and sixty thousand."

Aqua raised her head, nodded twice, and glared at the man who called himself Donny the Don. "I'm sure it is all here," she said. "Can't hurt to count it again, though. My daddy was a construction worker, and he'd always tell me to measure twice before I cut once. Simple advice, but it's helped a lot through life."

"Wise words, you ask me."

Aqua nodded her head a second time and continued to study Donny the Don through the eyeholes of her black cotton ski-mask. He had a round, handsome face, and he was dripping in designer gear. His rightward-leaning Gucci skullcap revealed a couple of braids and the chunky yellow diamond that pierced his left earlobe. His black leather Gucci gloves covered in the high-end designer's signature double G's, just like his heavy leather jacket and the turtleneck sweater he wore beneath it. He stood confidently in front of the three men and four women who'd helped him carry his nine duffle bags full of cash into the small west side apartment.

The young masked woman seated next Aqua, running a stack of hundreds through the second money counter, was Thick Doll. She danced with Aqua at Queen of Diamonds. So did Kimmy Kakes who was standing at the window with a Mini Draco pistol clutched in both hands, a burgundy ski-mask concealing her pretty brown face from Donny and his crew. Fat Perry, a bouncer at QOD, stood guard just inside the front door with a pistol in one chubby hand. A clique of Conservative Vice Lords were posted up in front of the apartment building with Glocks on their waists and murder in their eyes. The ruthless young gang members took orders directly from Thick Doll's stepfather, and tonight they'd been ordered to ensure her safety during this particular drug transaction.

If either member of Donny's little entourage made the wrong move, certain death would be sure to follow.

"You know," Donny said, snatching a glance at his diamond-flooded wristwatch, "most of my homies back home in Kankakee wouldn't dare come to Chicago with this much money. Niggas is scared of the Chi. They think all y'all do is gangbang and shoot each other. I had to tell one of my niggas the other day I been comin' here to cop my dope for the past eight or nine years and I ain't been robbed or shot yet."

"Lucky you," Thick Doll muttered snidely.

Danny gave her a look. "Yeah," he said, after a time. "Lucky me."

He went to the three cheap duffle bags Agua had left open on the equally tattered love seat to expose the twenty kilos of cocaine they contained. Ancient floorboards beneath the shit-brown carpeting creaked like elderly kneecaps as Donny crossed the room. He produced a keyring from his jacket pocket, stabbed a key into one of the bricks, and snorted some up his left nostril.

"Awww, yeah," he exclaimed, tipping his head back while at the same time nodding his approval. "This that shit right here. Woooo! Damn near came in my draws off that hit."

Aqua chuckled once and smiled through the mouth-hole of her mask. She would have laughed like the three young women in Danny's entourage if she wasn't feeling so nervous. Working as one of the most popular strippers in all of Chicago, she'd gotten fairly used to seeing and even taking home large sums of cash, so it wasn't the drug money that had her guts in a bunch. Neither was it due to all the guns in the room; this past summer she and her close friend Princess had begun visiting the shooting range quite frequently.

It was the twenty bricks of coke that had Talisha "Aqua" Mason's intestines coiling and twisting around each other like a boa constrictor in mating season.

I'm one of the most famous faces on television, she thought bitterly, *and yet here I sit, dealing kilos of cocaine like some kind of Mexican drug lord. Is this what my life's come to?*

She'd gotten herself into this predicament. There was no question about it. Way too much spending and not nearly enough saving. Her NBA star fiancé, Davion Carroll, had put a huge ten carat rock worth $2 million on her finger and deposited another $3 million in her bank account, and she'd foolishly blown through it all. Now she owned two Rolls Royce's and about a million dollars' worth of designer handbags. Her personal checking account balance was well below fifty grand, and her taste for the finer things in life had her credit card debt spiraling out of control. She enjoyed sucking Davion's dick about as much as she enjoyed holding her hand over an open flame, but here lately she'd been gulping down more sausage than Joey Chestnut, all in hopes of another seven-figure deposit to hold her over until the wedding next fall.

Then Davion's $300 million would be hers too.

She rubber-banded another stack of twenties and placed it inside the Burberry suitcase she had open on the floor next to her knee-high Balenciaga boots.

"Which one of y'all gave me that lap dance at the strip club the other week?" Donny the Don looked from Thick Doll to Aqua and back to Thick Doll. "That ass was so fat and soft and jiggly. Mmmm." He licked his lips and shook his head, lost in the reverie.

"It wasn't me," Thick Doll lied.

Aqua snickered at the lie and dropped a hefty stack of fifties into the money counter.

"I know it was one of them bad lil bitches from that MTN reality show." Donny said, zipping the coke-filled duffle bags shut and handing them off to the men in his clique. "It wasn't Princess or Aqua; I was fucked up that night, but I would've remembered if it was one of them. Them the baddest two lil bitches on the show."

Thick Doll and Kimmy Kakes sucked their teeth in unison, and Thick Doll rolled her eyes indignantly, eliciting another giggle from Aqua.

For the next fifteen minutes, the only sounds in the apartment came from the money counters and the Fox 32 newscast playing on the wall mounted television. It was November seventh, 2024. Half the country was still reeling over Trump's sweeping victory over Kamala Harris. Chicago drill rap superstar Lil Durk and several others in his crew had just been indicted for conspiracy to commit murder. A mass shooting had taken place on Monroe and Kildare. Two dead, three others wounded. There was snow on the ground, snow in the air, and more snow in the forecast. Still no Powerball winners. Better luck next time, America.

It was close to midnight when Donny the Don and his team left the apartment carrying six empty designer duffle bags and the three they had transferred the bricks into. All the cash didn't fit into Aqua's two Burberry suitcases, so she used the three cheap duffle bags to hold the rest of it. Keeping out only the $5,000 in fifties she'd promised to give Fat Perry for his role in the drug transaction.

Pushing her ski-mask up to the top of her head, Aqua inhaled deeply, exhaled dramatically, and reached out to Fat Perry with his cash in hand. "Here you go," she said, wiping a sheen of sweat from her forehead. "Thanks."

"Bitch, you got me fucked up," he snapped.

Aqua jerked back in surprise.

Fat Perry snatched off his mask and took three steps toward Aqua, his heavy footfalls shaking the entire living room. "Bitch," he repeated and this time a line of spittle formed along his lower lip. "I just stood here and watched y'all count out over half a million dollars. I need more than five thousand."

"People in hell need ice-water." Thick Doll countered. "You can't always get what you want. Now move your fat ass out the way so we can go."

Fat Perry was, as the name implied, a very fat man. He stood maybe an inch shy of six feet tall and weighed maybe an ounce shy of two hundred-eighty pounds. His eyebrows were like overweight caterpillars over his beady eyes. He glowered down at Aqua and Thick Doll. If his size wasn't intimidating enough, the 5.56-millimeter AR pistol he was holding down by his side did the trick.

Especially when he raised it to Aqua's face.

Moving the gun barrel from Aqua to Thick Doll and back again, he delivered a strong-voiced ultimatum: "Either you give me *FIFTY* thousand outta there or I'm takin' *ALL* of it! Now what it's gon' be?"

"See?" Thick Doll extended an arm toward Fat Perry, her French-tipped fingernails pointing up toward his immensely unattractive face. "Didn't I tell you not to bring this nigga in on this? This hundred-dollar a night ass nigga; he ain't never had no fuckin' money."

Aqua's heartbeat hastened. She swung an arm out to her side, sweeping Karionna "Thick Doll" Washington behind her before her unfiltered rants could get them both killed.

"Listen Perry," Aqua said placidly, "this money belongs to the plug. Okay? It's not mine. I only get a small percentage of this money, and I'm splitting it evenly between the four of us. Now if you wanna get greedy and rob us all, go ahead. I can't stop you. But just know that you'll be taking from one of Weezy's best friends. They ain't gon' wanna hear no excuses."

Fat Perry hesitated. His beady eyes darted from Aqua's nervous smile to the pile of fifties in her hand. Finally, he took the cash from her with one great swipe of his mammoth paw.

Seconds later the four of them were descending the dark stairwell, Aqua and Thick Doll rolling the suitcases behind them, Kimmy Kakes carrying all three of the duffels. They were in an apartment building on Karlov Avenue, not all that far from where tonight's so-called mass shooting took place. Thick Doll's cousin Pat rented the apartment they had used for the drug deal.

"This shit far from over," Thick Doll muttered when Fat Perry was far enough ahead of them and on the staircase. "If he think I'm just gon' let him get away with pointing a gun in my face he got another thing coming."

"Let's just make it out of here first," Aqua said shakily.

They made it outside, and the cold air smacked Aqua like a heavy-handed pimp. Mook, the leader of the pack of wolves, gathered in front of the building, licked his chapped lips and blew a kiss at Aqua. He grabbed his crotch and shook his dreads while his boys moved aside.

"Shorty, you thick than a bitch," someone said.

"On gang. That's Kari in the middle. You know she strip at QOD's. Them other two lil bops prolly strip too."

"Man, that's shorty n'em from *The Real Bad Bitches of Chicago*. On fo'nem, that lil light-skinned bitch fuck wit' a basketball player. Shorty, you supposed to be laid up in a mansion somewhere. The fuck is you doin' out here in the trenches!"

Aqua ignored the voices and trailed Fat Perry out the wrought-iron gate and onto the sidewalk. He went to his ten-year-old Buick sedan, while Kari led the way to the rear of Aqua's cream white Navigator. Mook and another dreadhead he called Tails came out and helped load the suitcases and duffle into the rear storage compartment.

"Who was buddy in the Benz truck?" Mook asked Kari as Aqua secured the rear door.

She didn't stick around to hear Thick Doll's answer, namely because a flurry of snowflakes were stinging her eyes, but also because she didn't trust Mook and his gang. Most of them were staring at her fat round ass, or at Kimmy's fat wide ass, or at Kari's fat bubble butt, but they were also glancing from one end of the block to the other end, as if they expected trouble of some sort.

So Aqua hurried around to her driver door and got in. Kimmy got in next to her a few seconds later. Like Aqua, she had tied her hair up in a topknot before putting on her mask, and now she busied herself in the visor mirror, taking a comb from her oversized Chanel bag and using it to get her expensive lace front wig in order.

Getting her own do back together was the furthest thing from Aqua's mind. A CPD squad car turned off Thomas Street and went trundling past, followed closely by a brown Chevy van. Aqua held her breath until the pigs were out of sight; pigs that were ironically threatening enough to send a few of Mooks wolves scurrying off into the gangway next to Kari's cousin Pat's building.

"Shit," Aqua said, and dropped her forehead against the upper curvature of her steering wheel. Her hands trembled. Her heart was a piston in her chest. "What the hell is Karionna doing back there?"

"Still talking to Mook. You know they used to mess around. The nigga got a foot fetish. As a matter of fact, they broke up when she found out he had paid Cherish Taylor five hundred dollars for a foot job."

"Five hundred dollars for a foot job," Kimmy said nodding and smiling with amusement. "He put his dick between her feet and she, like jacked him off... with her feet."

"I'm done." Aqua reconnected her brow with the steering wheel, snickering in her throat. "I'm so done with this night."

After a moment, she sat up and started the engine. Got the heat going. Pressed play on Chris Brown's "Under the Influence" and cranked the volume up a couple of notches. She was rubbing the palms of her hands on the thighs of her blue jeans and contemplating whether she'd use her share of the drug money to pay down her credit card debt or cop herself another Hermes Birkin bag when the boy named Tails appeared outside her window.

He grinned and signaled for her to lower her window, and when she shook her head no his grin grew into a smile that revealed several chipped teeth.

"I ain't tryna bother you, shorty. On bro. I just wanna get a picture with you for my sister. She in the hospital fightin' cancer right now, and her favorite two shows to watch is *Chicago PD* and that stripper show you on."

Damn. He'd hit her right in the gut with that one.

Reluctantly, she lowered her window an inch. "I, uhh... I don't wanna take no pics. Not tonight, anyway." She picked up her iPhone from the center console. "Is your sister on IG?"

Tails nodded and gave Aqua his sister's Instagram name. Martisha Miller. She looked tall as a tree and thin as a stick. She was four or five shades darker than her brother, with dimpled cheeks and a smooth bald head she kept covered in a bonnet in most pictures.

Despite having over five million followers, Aqua had followed back just three hundred and twenty-eight when she hit follow on Martisha's page.

"Thanks," Tails said, just as Kari was pulling open the rear passengers' side door and climbing in. He flashed another warm smile offering a second glimpse of his jagged teeth. His dreads were twisted into fat braids, so that they resembled black and gold Twizzlers trapped behind his Gucci headband. His heavy leather Pelle-Pelle coat was red like Aqua's Balenciaga hoodie. He nodded his thanks, gave her sideview mirror a gentle slap, and turned to rejoin his gang on the sidewalk, looking toward Thomas Street as a set of blinding white headlights swept onto Karlov from that direction.

Instinctively, Aqua looked in her sideview mirror. The brown Chevy van was back, going just two or three miles per hour this time. Creeping through the snowfall.

"Mook was just telling me about that shit that went down over there on Monroe. Guess who did that shit?" Kari said

No guesses were made, because at that very moment just as Aqua was shifting into drive and Fat Perry was pulling away from the curb ahead of them, a pair of masked gunmen leapt out of the Chevy van and opened fire on Mook and his gang.

Aqua ducked low and let loose a piercing scream.

"Bitch, you better go! Drive!" Kari yelled.

Flinching and wincing at the barrage of gunfire, Aqua raised her head just enough to see the road ahead and stomped down on the gas pedal, launching her navigator forward and side-swiping Fat Perry's car as she raced past him.

Chapter 1

"I'd really hate to have to fuck you up, Weezy, but you know I will, so please don't tempt me."

Weezy's round, pudgy face lit up in a fat-cheeked smile as he looked up from his computer and stared at the woman who'd aided him in making Queen of Diamonds the most lucrative gentlemen's club in the Windy City.

Her given name was Gabrielle Guy, but everybody and their mama called her Big Gabby. For a long time, the "Big" had been due to her obesity— she'd once tipped the scale at three hundred and twenty-nine pounds. Then came Ozempic. The miracle weight loss drug, coupled with a muscled up physical trainer and a major shift in her diet, had shaved a lot of fat off her bones. Now she was a still a bit on the heavy side, but the meaning behind the "Big" had changed. Now it was more of a status symbol, similar to the way Atlanta rap phenom Mulatto had gradually become known as Big Latto. Now it was *Big* Gabby, CFO of Whips Out Lingerie and the owner of five franchise restaurants. Now it was *Big* Gabby, Chief Operating Officer and House Mom at the Queen of Diamonds, the boss bitch who'd held down the fort while Weezy was away in Malibu, California receiving physical therapy for his hand that had been severed and then reattached following a sword attack earlier in the year, and boy was she glad to see him back behind his desk, dressed in one of the teeth-clenching expensive three-piece business suits he was known for wearing and smiling his wide, open-mouthed smile.

"I see you done went and slimmed down on me," he said, easing back in his swivel chair and interlacing his fingers behind his shiny bald head. "Lookin' like a bag o'money. What you done lost, forty, fifty pounds?"

"More like seventy-five. I really could've lost more, but I had some of the fat transferred to my ass. One can never really have too much junk in the trunk, you feel me?"

Roy "Weezy" Sullivan threw his head back and bellowed out a stentorian laugh that didn't sound much like a laugh at all. It was more like one long shout. *HAAA!* That was the sound. It made Big Gabby giggle as she smacked her newly manicured claws onto her jumbo butt cheeks and did a slow spin in her tight white Dolce and Gabbana dress, showing off her jiggly goods.

"Yeeeahh," she said. "Mikayla ain't got ass like *this*, do she?"

Another long, shouting laugh from Weezy. "I ain't seen or talked to that bitch in three or four months. Bossed her up and let her go. That's the way you do it."

Big Gabby gave a nod and went to one of the two plush leather armchairs in front of Weezy's desk. She sat down and moved around a little, getting comfortable. The ice on her neck and wrists twinkled a rainbow of colors. Weezy ran a hand down his face and rolled forward in his chair, and Gabby knew he was ready to get down to business.

"So what I done missed since the last time we talked? What's goin' on with the girls?"

Big Gabby shrugged. "Same-o, same-o. We lost five girls to Redbone's and three others to Club Ocean, gained twelve more. I promoted Kitty Jae and Gold Body to Prime Shift. Trying to get Princess to put them on that TV show, but you know she's all bougie now. She quit dancing and everything. I heard she got twelve million to produce The Real Baddies, and you know Markio's spoiling the shit out of her. They got her thinking she's the new Shaunie O'Neal. Plus, you know she's real tight with Alexus now, and that *really* got her feeling herself."

"What about her lil friend?" Weezy looked at his computer, took hold of the mouse, and clicked his way to the camera system.

"Aqua's off tonight. So is Thick Doll, and Kimmy Kakes called in sick. I think they up to something. Last night, when I was going over the parking lot camera, I saw the three of them all huddled up next to Aqua's truck. Fat Perry was standing there with 'em. I intended to ask him what was going on when he came in tonight, but guess what?"

"That nigga called in sick too," Weezy guessed.

"That nigga called in sick too," Big Gabby echoed. "I'm telling you, something's up. I'm interrogating Fat Perry's sneaky ass when he gets in tomorrow afternoon. I might even—"

Weezy waved off Big Gabby's intimidating tactics with the hand he'd briefly lost to the blade of an old man's cane sword. The fingers of that hand were curled a little. The surgical scar lay hidden beneath the rose gold band of his Rolex watch.

"You can get more flies with sugar than you can with shit," he said, eyeing the cameras again. "Put one of the girls on him. He'll tell everything." Wrinkling his forehead, he leaned toward the computer screen, maneuvering his mouse to zoom in on the VIP Lounge. "Who this we got in VIP?"

"Depends on which table you're talking about."

Weezy turned his computer monitor so Big Gabby could see it and pointed his slightly bent forefinger at the table in question. There stood a group of seven men, all of them wearing black hoodies with the same photo printed on the chests and the same blue words printed on their backs. Half a dozen black bottles of Bel Air Rose' littered their table; alongside several blocks of cash and what looked like Backwoods cigarillo wrappers. The men were smoking and passing around blunts, drinking from bottles and Styrofoam cups, throwing fistfuls of dollars at the four big-bootied Prime shift dancers who'd come over to entertain them.

"Oh," Big Gabby said. "That's Bowlegs and his guys from the Low End. The Hobos, I think they're called. It says 'The Earth is our Turf' on the back of their hoodies, and 'Rest in Peace Keytron' on the front. From what I heard down in the locker room, the Hobos run a dope line on 47th and Vincennes and two more somewhere on 51st. Shmoney Rose said they're beefing with the Fifth Ward Black Disciples— you know them, Black Ant and Flem and their guys from off 45th and Capitol. Remember they celebrated Flem's birthday here the first week we opened."

Weezy's gaping smile made a swift return. His eyes rolled sideways and settled on Big Gabby, but his gleaming bald head didn't move an inch. "You know who that is, right?" His voice was raspy and deep, as if it had begun its vocal journey in the soles of his size sixteen feet and made the six feet, nine-inch climb to the top of his skull before dropping back down to swing out of his cavernous, alcohol-scented mouth. "Keytron, I mean. You don't remember that name? Keytron Douglas? Died in that double homi down there on 60th and Hermitage?"

Big Gabby's long faux eyelashes came together in a thoughtful squint. She lowered her head and picked a spot of lint off her eight-thousand-dollar dress. *Keytron Douglas*, she thought. The name rang a bell. *Double homicide on 60th and Hermitage?* She ruminated over it a moment longer, mouth twisted, staring vacantly at the flawless white diamonds in her Cartier watch…

Then she gasped and sat up, her eyes becoming as wide and round as her open lips.

"Those boys Princess shot when they ran up on her ex! The other boy's name was Donte Edgebrook!" Big Gabby rose to her feet, excited. "You think the Hobos are here to send a message to Princess? I mean, it has to be a message to her, right? Her ex is in jail."

"Not no more, he ain't. Folks just got out today. Shorty he got jammed up with took the case."

"What was his name again?"

"Grind. He's one of the guys from off 69th and Lowe. All that shit started when two of the Hobos tried to rob Grind. He shot both of them and ended up gettin' charged with two counts of attempted murder, and when I bonded him out Bowlegs sent Keytron and Donte to whack Folks. I guess ol 'Princess was quicker on the draw."

"Should I call and warn her?"

Weezy stood up, shaking his head. "Nah," he said, with a conspiratorial smirk. "She'll be aight. I'm sure she'll get word of it eventually. That nigga Bowlegs gon' make sure of that."

Chapter 2

With her hands planted firmly on her knees and her big wobbly ass bouncing along to the beat of Dreezy's latest club banger, Jaresha "Kitty Jae" Brady was the center of attention in QOD's exclusive VIP Lounge. She was a redbone, five feet seven inches tall and a hundred seventy-five pounds of mouthwatering curves. An avid fan of horror films, she had an array of scary movie villains inked into her skin from the ankle of her left leg up to her waist, and from the wrist of her left arm up to her shoulders. Poor Jason Voorhees, who had the supreme misfortune of being tatted on her left but cheek, had suffered a vast number of messy cumshots to his hockey mask. Like the other girls of Prime Shift, Kitty Jae was an impossibly beautiful young woman, and she could bounce her ass and wiggle her thighs like no one else in the building.

She stood up straight, making her fat butt cheeks jump up and down as she looked back at the man who'd introduced himself as Paris. He was skinny, maybe six-two in height, and Kitty Jae might have considered him handsome if not for the slight squint to his left eye.

"Shake that fat muthafucka," he said, and nibbled at the center of his bottom lip as he smacked Jason Voorhees with a stack of one dollar bills.

Kitty Jae shook that fat muthafucka. Behind her, Paris and his boy Bowlegs started up a chant— *Ay-ay-ay* like OJ Da Juiceman. There were several more Prime Shift girls shaking what their mamas and surgical doctor gave them to shake.

Cherish Taylor, Shmoney Rose, Bunny XXX, Sasha the Stallion, Plinni Munni, and the repulsively annoying yet stunningly attractive Blicky Nicky. Collectively they were known as the Prime Time Girls, or PTG for short. Cherish, Plinni Munni, and Sasha the Stallion were entertaining the Hobos with Kitty Jae, while across the room, the other girls danced beneath a hurricane of dollar bills thrown by Weezy's cousin Big Boy and his squad of Black Disciples from off 69th Street and Emerald Avenue.

A thin thread of envy needled its way into Kitty Jae's heart as she glanced in Big Boy's direction. The fat man had arrived with ten of his boys, and he'd paid for three tables at five hundred dollars each. He had a good ten or fifteen grand piled up on the three tables, cash that had drawn in a few pretty girls who weren't dancers, and a jubilant line of bottle girls had marched up the steps to bring Big Boy and his gang over two dozen bottles of champagne.

Meanwhile, the Hobos occupied just one table, and they only had about two thousand dollars in singles to blow. Big Boy and his boys wore enough diamond jewelry to supply a small jewelry store, while only two members of the Hobos wore any jewelry at all.

Kitty Jae was able to smile through the disappointment. Thursday nights were always kind of slow. She would go home with fifteen or sixteen hundred, more than enough to pay up all her bills and get her boyfriend the two pairs of Jordans he wanted for his upcoming birthday. She'd be broke afterward, but that would change after this weekend. QOD's VIP Lounge was always loaded with celebrities on the weekends, and only the Prime Time Girls were allowed in VIP during Prime Shift which ran from 10:00 PM to 2:00 AM This weekend's lineup of musical performances included Quavo, Big Boogie, and Moneybagg Yo, and since the performers were routinely comped a table in VIP, Kitty Jae and the rest of the PTG were destined to rake up at least ten to fifteen grand a piece by the end of the weekend. Kitty

Jae would use that money for Christmas and more. She'd worry about her sisters and their kids next week, her parents and grandparents the week after that, and maybe she'd sit down sometime in December and figure out how she was going to pay back the six figure business loan she owed to Bank of America.

Many of her money woes could be gone whenever Weezy returned to his office, and not because of the iced-out Cuban-link necklace and fifty-thousand-dollar pile of Benjamins she expected him to gift her for proving herself. Worthy of becoming an official Prime Time Girl.

The remedy to Kitty Jae's financial trouble resided in the age-spotted hands of the eighty-year-old Vietnam war veteran who'd drawn a sword from inside his walking cane and lopped off Weezy's hand in one sweeping stroke. The old man had approached her with this exciting proposition on a warm morning in June, back when she was a struggling dancer at Redbone's and her stage name was Jardi B. She answered her doorbell and found the charcoal black man standing there on her front porch, smoking a cigarette and examining his yellowing fingernails. Two similarly complected women who appeared to be in their early to mid-twenties were standing behind him, one of them swiping a fingertip up the screen of her iPhone, the other silently studying a white Cadillac that was riding down Millard Avenue. All three of them had turned to look at Kitty Jae.

"I think y'all got the wrong house." Kitty Jae had said, pulling her Dior bathrobe closed.

"I think we got the right one," the old man replied, his voice at least eight times raspier than any voice she'd ever heard before then. "Jaresha Brady, right? Linda Wright's youngest child, and Cecil Brady's only daughter, am I right?"

Kitty Jae had squinted at the elderly fellow, and when he reached out with that age-spotted, leathery old hand, she took it in hers and gave it a slow, reluctant shake.

21

"Herbert Harris. Nice day to make a friend, wouldn't you say? How'd you like to make a half a million dollars?"

Now, as she went to the chromium pole that stood between the Hobos' crowded VIP able and the vacant table next to it, Kitty Jae tried without much success to erase the memory of that seemingly friendly front porch conversation from wherever it lived in her brain.

She took hold of the pole and did a provocative spin around it, lowering into a squat and making her right booty cheek jump again and again while the left one stood still. She wore only a black fishnet cat suit and five-inch Chanel wedges of the same color and there were dollars of every denomination stuck behind the netted strings. Her hair was done in a jet black, shoulder length bob. Her nipples were hard not because of the cool air blowing down from the overhead ventilation but because she had snorted a line of coke in the Prime Shift locker room less than an hour ago. And cocaine always made her horny.

She stood up, holding the pole in both hands, leaning back, and winding her hips as she stuck her tongue out at Bowlegs, the man who was clearly the main breadwinner in this particular group of Hobos. He was short and stocky, his HOBO tattoo covered the whole frontside of his muscular neck, and as his name implied he had legs that bowed out to the sides like Kitty Jae's hips. She turned her back to him, bent forward with her hands cupping her D-cups and stepped back until a considerable length of the steel pole disappeared between her butt cheeks.

The two staircases leading up to the VIP Lounge were both roped off, and the entire section was glassed in, glass that Big Gabby fiercely demanded be cleaned three times a day, at eight-hour intervals. Looking out through the clean glass and down at the main floor below, Kitty Jae was mildly surprised to see that the club was still crammed full of people.

It was mostly a black crowd: hood bitches and street niggas, blunt smokers and Lean sippers, old school players and savage young gang members. Some were tax-paying citizens, some weren't. Kitty jae spotted a clique of girls she'd grown up with in North Lawndale, several hustlers and gangsters she knew from all across the city, and one handsome college boy she'd politely turned down at a party two years ago because she thought he might be gay. The college boy was tall, skinny, and dark skinned just like the old man Herbert Harris.

"All you gotta do," Herb had said in that eerily raspy voice, *"is give me a ring the next time Weezy show his face in that club he owns over there on 73rd and Cottage and let me know what kind of car he's driving. You do that and the money's all yours."*

Kitty Jae had regarded him with a disbelieving side-eye. Then the girl holding the iPhone had offered to show her the cash. She'd walked Kitty Jae to the blacked-out Bentley Mulsanne one of them had parked at the curb behind Kitty Jae's gray 2008 Tahoe, popped the trunk, and showed her the stacks upon stacks of hundreds they had stuffed in a black leather duffle bag.

Seventeen days later while auditioning to become a Preferred Shift dancer at Queen of Diamonds, Jardi B became Kitty Jae—coined after Kitty Rae White, some chick Big Gabby swore she bore a striking resemblance to—and the rest was history. Kitty Jae went from making five or six hundred dollars a night at Redbone's to averaging five or six thousand dollars a night at Queen of Diamonds; from pushing a sixteen year old Tahoe with almost two hundred thousand miles on the odometer to driving a 2024 Mercedes Benz G wagon that was fresh off the assembly line; from living with her older brother, her two younger sisters, and their four badass children in their mother's building on 16th Street and Millard Avenue to actually buying the house next door and allowing her two sisters—twenty three year old

Daimeka Wright and eighteen year old, batshit -crazy Shalonda Wright to move into the second floor apartment. Worst decision ever. (*Thump- thump-thump* all through the day.) She'd even managed to coerce the executives at Bank of America into loaning her the money needed to buy the McDonald's restaurant that sat at the corner of Roosevelt Road and Kedzie Avenue. Sure, Shalonda had burned it down within the first few weeks of business.

"See, if you would've just gave me that eight thousand dollars I asked you for," the nutcase had reasoned, "this shit wouldn't have happened." Hence the six-figure debt Kitty Jae now owed to her bank, but a part of her still viewed the failed business venture as a success.

After all, who in her family was well off enough to get a $195,000 bank loan in the first place?

Kitty Jae had zoned out on the pole, spinning and climbing and doing splits, all the while making her ass clap and her thighs wiggle. She didn't snap out of it until she looked up and saw two more groups of people being led into the VIP Lounge.

She gasped and stumbled a little when she realized that the man leading the way was none other than Roy "Weezy" Sullivan.

Chapter 3

"So tell me," Alexus Costilla said, fingering a lock of long, silky black hair from in front of her gorgeous bronze face. "What are your plans for the season finale? Are you thinking classy or are you thinking of something more… ratchet?"

"Ratchet," Princess replied, without a moment's hesitation. "Definitely ratchet."

Alexus tilted her head to the side and laughed. Whiskey slashed around in her low-ball glass but settled before any could spill over the rim, which was a good thing, because as the devilishly handsome waiter had explained as he poured, the drink was a whiskey collector's wet dream. At $150,000 a bottle, from a Japanese distillery that no longer existed, the sherry barrel aged 1965 vintage single malt Karuizawa 50-year-old was practically unobtainable.

But then again, when you were Alexus Costilla-King, not only the CEO of the Minority Television Network but also the only person in human history to ever accumulate a net worth that exceeded a quarter of a trillion dollars—*TMZ* had broken the news of this remarkable milestone just yesterday— nothing in the world was really unobtainable, was it?

To celebrate the unprecedented milestone, Queen A was hosting an All-White party inside downtown Chicago's stylishly decadent new Costilla Hotel & Tower. She and her many, many celebrity friends were gathered in the 19,000 square-foot rooftop lounge—"The largest in the state!" she proclaimed a moment earlier—and now as Princess Kelly stood with her own ball glass of liquor in one hand and her titanium backed iPhone in the other, wearing a skintight Louis Vuitton bandage wrap dress and lambskin booties that were as blindingly white as the designer fabrics everyone else wore, she couldn't think of a single time in her life when she'd felt more out of place.

"Drink up," Alexus said. "Let your hair down and live a little. You look like you've seen a ghost."

"I'm fine." It was a lie, but it came out stoutly enough. Of course, she couldn't tell what her face was showing. "I'm just trying to figure out where's the place to film that finale. I want it to be just as explosive as the episode was in Costa Rica."

"I thought Aqua was actually going to push Shmoney Rose over that balcony. I know *I* would've. Bitch would've had me too fucked up." Alexus uttered another laugh. She was cheery-eyed and at that moment looked much younger than her thirty-two years.

Princess tried on a smile that didn't quite fit and took a considerably large swallow from her glass. The cognac sluiced down her throat like boiling hot lava. She'd opted for Hennesy. Like the title of that old Nikki Turner novel, Princess Kelly was a project chick, and project chicks drank Henny. It hit her in her chest just behind her surgically enhanced melons and then spread out from there like internal peace and joy. And allowing her to accept the fact that yes, she really *had* just taken a selfie with Chris Brown, who'd casually slipped one tattooed arm around her lower back and smilingly complimented her outfit just before she snapped the picture. And yes, she really had just accepted welcoming hugs from LeBron, Angel Reese, Kevin Hart, Viola Davis, and Michael B. Jordan, as well as several other slightly less impressive introductions that were equally unforgettable.

And yes, that really *was* Beyonce standing on the opposite side of Alexus, talking and laughing and having a genuinely good time with Jennifer Hudson and Adele. It was the latter reality that had Princess looking like she'd seen a ghost. No wonder she and everyone else had been asked to sign non-disclosure agreements before gaining entry to this extravagant affair. No wonder there was such a heavy security presence, with white-suited men and women in dark sunglasses posted in every corner and at every exit like sentries.

Amazing what two hundred and fifty billion dollars could get you. Just like Queen Bey, Alexus Costilla had also scored herself a billionaire rap husband. He was Blake King, known all around the globe as Bulletface, and right now he and Bey's hubby were huddled a couple of feet to the left of Prinny, kicking the shit with Lil Wayne, Nicki Minaj, Mellow Rackz, and 2 Chains.

There was enough star power in the building to light up the whole city.

Alexus enjoyed her whiskey in small sips, making it last, but Prinny slugged hers like a college freshman. It wasn't enough to get her drunk, but it took away some of the anxiety and loosened her up a bit, enough to make her remember and revel in the comforting fact that she herself was a star among stars. Princess Kelly was not just the producer of the #1 show on Primetime television, she was also one of the show's three *executive* producers. It said so right there in the opening credits of every episode of *The Real Baddies of Chicago*—which had been unceremoniously changed from *The Real Bad Bitches of Chicago* "for marketing purposes," according to MTN's board of executives.

Prinny was no billionaire, but she was indeed a multimillionaire, raking in a helluva lot more than she'd ever made as a dancer at Queen of Diamonds.

Not bad for a project chick.

Her phone buzzed in her hand hardly a minute after Jeezy and Bulletface took to the stage in the middle of the lounge to perform *Snowstorm*, a classic trap anthem off Bulletface's *The White Album*, an album that had gone diamond and added two more Grammys to his already extensive collection.

"I really have to take this call," Prinny said as she and Alexus trekked toward the stage with a crowd of others. This was another lie. In all honesty, she had no idea who was calling her from the unfamiliar 773 number.

"Okay," Alexus said. "But hurry up. Bey's performing next. She brought background dancers, and I think one of 'em is Blue. I'd literally *die* if I missed even a second of that."

She made a beeline for the women's room, ditching her empty glass along the way and traversing the floor easily enough. She had to pee. *Bad.* Her bladder overfloweth. She'd sucked down two sixteen-ounce Poland spring waters to cure herself of the cottonmouth she'd gotten from smoking a blunt of exotic bud with her sister, Kamari, before leaving out for Alexus's star-studded event. Now she was about ready to spring a leak.

"Please God, don't let me piss on myself in front of all these people." She muttered under her breath as she moved hastily toward the restrooms, skirting around the Kardashian sisters and an actress she'd seen in one of MTN's low budget holiday movies. "I've come way too far in this short little TV career to go out as Little Miss Pee Body."

She clenched her teeth and forged ahead, trying to keep her notably long strides cute, while at the same time checking her cell phone and wondering who was calling her. Had it been from an out-of-town area code she'd have sent the caller straight to voicemail. But it was a local number. It could be family or an old friend. Or one of the girls Big Gabby had promoted to Prime Shift in hopes of getting them added to the cast of The Read Baddies.

When she was closing in on the ladies room, with nothing between her and the door but seven feet of empty space, Prinny closed her eyes for two short seconds and saw a vision of nightmare clarity— a yellow wet spot forming at the lower front part of her dress, widening and lengthening in a downward trajectory, and when she looks up to see if anybody looking, she finds herself standing alone on the stage she'd just seen Bulletface and Jeezy standing on, and everybody's looking, pointing and laughing.

She opened her eyes and ran quickly before any shred of that horrifying vision could come to fruition. In through the door with the reflective steel plate at the bottom, across the spotless black marble floor, and into the open door of the second stall. She threw the door shut, engaged the lock, hiked up her dress, and squatted over the high-tech smart toilet.

Her pretty brown eyes rolled up in her head, and she let out a long, relaxing breath as the stream shot out of her.

"Oh thank you Jesus," she said, panting.

Someone yodeled laughter in the next stall over. Prinny smirked and blew a nasal sigh of relief. Finishing up, she unshouldered her white croc skin Birkin bag, dug out a flushable wet wipe, and used it to cleanse any traces of that great flood from her slit before flushing and leaving the stall.

At the sink, her phone rang again. Same number.

"Who is this?" she eyed her reflection in the mirror as she answered the call. An errant lack of blond hair lay on her chocolate brown forehead and she looked extraordinarily beautiful, even more visually appealing, some might argue, than the ice filled Tiffany necklace she wore around her slender neck, and the matching set of earrings and bracelets.

"Don't hang up," said the man on the other end of the phone line.

Prinny's expression hardened. It was Vincent Rose, AKA Grind— the tall, ruggedly handsome man she'd dated for a short time last year. He was a Gangster Disciple from

Englewood. A drug dealer who knew how to stack his money and how to treat his woman. Princess had reciprocated the love, fucking and sucking him like Mimi Faust, allowing him into the Highland Park mansion she and her younger sister Kamari had purchased not long before they began dating. She'd given him twenty-five thousand dollars to reup on the pills he sold, and when he was arrested on two counts of attempted murder for shooting two Hobos who tried robbing him for those pills, Princess had dropped another fifteen grand on a lawyer. On top of all that, when he made bail a few weeks later and those two masked gunmen ran up on him seconds after she and Grind had pulled up outside his sister's house in her Benz, Princess had drawn her Glock and shot them dead.

And how had he repaid her?

"You dirty-ass bitch," Prinny said glowering. "What did you do, bribe some guard into bringing you a cell phone?"

"Nahh. They dismissed that gun charge, and I beat them two attempts. Paris and Jonesy didn't show up for trial. They freed me at around three o'clock this afternoon."

Behind her, the door to the stall next to the one she'd used swung inward, and the narrow bodied woman from Tyler Perry's *Sistas*—the one who'd been pregnant for a thousand and one days it seemed— walked out wearing an amused smile over a sheer white blouse and slacks. Prinny's mouth-dropped open, and for the umpteenth time tonight she found herself starstruck. She told Grind quite belligerently to hold on for a second as she raised her free hand and gave the approaching actress a small, meaningful wave.

"I *love* your show," Prinny said. "I've been a fan since season one. I was actually rooting for you and Zack in the beginning, way back before Fatima was even a factor."

"Girl, I love your show, too. *The Real Baddies* is my jam. Our group chat goes crazy during and after every episode. We are so proud of you. Congrats on your success."

Prinny's heart swelled with a particular kind of joy—the kind that comes with tears hidden somewhere beneath it. She thanked the petite young actress, then watched her wash and dry her hands and leave the bathroom in a heel clicking hurry, no doubt eager to catch the rest of Jeezy and Bulletface's performance.

Shifting her attention back to Grind, she plucked her AirPods out of her purse, stuck them in her ears and said, "Grind, I trusted you. I trusted you! I *killed* for you! And what did I get in return? You accepting Weezy's money to harm me over some bullshit extortion scheme I had nothing to do with? You showing up outside my house with a fucking *gun* on your lap? And now you got the nerrrve to get outta jail and call *me*?"

"Listen, I apologize for that, but I was not about to hurt you. I would *never* do anything to hurt you. And that's on everything I love. As a matter of fact, I was 'bout to get down on buddy who was in the truck with me, but twelve pulled up, and we got arrested before I could do it." He paused, as if expecting her to speak. When she didn't, he continued. "I'm only calling to warn you. I know buddy n'em you shot was some Mickey Cobras, but they was related to Bowlegs, and he's... Well, you might as well say he's the chief of the Hobos, even though technically they ain't really got no chief."

Grind paused again and got a second dose of silence from Princess Kelly. Still scowling truculently, she turned to get a side view of her huge bubble butt in the mirror; it was so fat she had to wrestle her dress back down over it a few moments ago.

"Anyway," Grind said, sounding frustrated, "they all up in VIP at Queen of Diamonds right now— Paris, Bowlegs, and all the rest o'dem niggas. They went there to find you, but only 'cause of me. They know I just got out. I would slide through there myself, try and catch them niggas leaving out, but I ain't got nothing. My big sister and her dope fiend ass boyfriend ran off with everything I had. All my money. All my pistols I ain't got shit."

"Cry me a whole goddam river. Karma's a bad bitch in high heels, and you won't get a lick of sympathy from me. Shouldn't have went to jail, bitch. You deserve every stroke of bad luck you can get."

"Whatever." Grind's frustration had become something much more fiery and aggressive. "I need to swing by yo' spot and grab that bookbag I left over there. I need that bread I left in there. That's all I got to my name. "

"Psshh," Prinny scoffed. "That's over with. Did you forget that you owed me forty thousand dollars before you went to jail? You only had sixty-two thousand in that bag. That other twenty-two stacks is mine too. Call it accrued interest. Fuck you and have a nice day." She hit the END CALL button before he could get another word in, considered blocking his number, then decided against it and silenced her phone ringer instead. Grind called back immediately, and Prinny sent him straight to voicemail, the overcrowded graveyard where the deeply apologetic words of all the people who were dead to her resided. A part of her wanted to believe–*needed t*o believe—that Grind wasn't the backstabbing snake she's believed him to be ever since that day she had watched him get taken into custody right outside her home, but she knew that was probably just some inner emotion, still tethered to him by the thinnest of strings. She would return that tan leather backpack to him with every dollar that was in it when he left it with her last year. That whole Deebo spiel had been all bark, no bite; Prinny wasn't a thief. And then she would go home to the man who'd taken Grind's place.

Millionaire Markio.

Shouldering her purse, Prinny went to the miles-long thread of text messages between her and Markio and typed out a quick one.

You bett not be sleep when I get home. If you is I'm waking you up with that slurp, slurp.
She ended the text with a tongue-out emoji, snapped half a dozen mirror selfies, and selected the most bootylicious one to send with the message.

Then, with a contented smile, she pinched the hem of her dress and yanked it down over her bountiful buttocks once more before she went sauntering out of the restroom just as the opening notes to Beyonce's *1+1* began pulsing through the lounge.

Chapter 4

Princess Kelly wasn't the only Prime Time Girl dealing with an unwanted caller.

Gazing down at the screen of her iPhone with a look that suggested more weariness than defiance, Aqua pressed the END CALL button for the fifth time in ten minutes.

"If this man calls me one more time, I swear to God," she said taking her forehead in one hand and squeezing. "I just might beat him upside his head with one of my shoes next time I see him."

It was Fat Perry calling, demanding another five grand for the damage she'd done to his car in her haste to escape the Karlove Avenue shooting.

"Don't stress yourself out over that bum," Thick Doll said dismissively. "He knows you're a naïve little schoolgirl from way out of Joliet. That's the only reason he's trying you like that. He is a straight up lame. He used to sell packs for my step-daddy, Yella Man, but Yella had to cut him off 'cause he kept getting robbed. He tried to flex with the PPP loan and got stung for the twenty thousand. Them BD's took his dumbass out to Parkway Gardens and stripped him butt ass naked. Made him walk like eight blocks, and it was raining, too."

The mental image of a stark-naked Fat Perry, shuffling down O Block with his substantial belly rocking from side to side in front of him, sent Aqua into a raucous fit of laughter.

She and Thick doll were alone in a room so cavernous that it required a trio of chandeliers and three marquetry coffee tables which were custom made in Bali by Etienne de Souza, to keep it from looking empty. The original blueprints called it a ballroom, and Aqua still referred to it as such, but she'd had her interior designer decorate it as a large space for gatherings. On either side of its cream-colored limestone fireplace were shelves, crafted from eucalyptus wood, which displayed a vast collection of books, back issues of JET, Ebony, Essence, and XXL, and just about every board game in existence. There were enough square-edged white Minotti sofas for the whole gang to be seated and Thick Doll had taken to one of them as if it was her own bed, lying supine with an erotic Zane novel spread open on the belly of the black Chanel bathrobe she borrowed from Aqua's studio apartment-sized closet after showering. The robe was parted just enough to show the full swells of her perfect breasts, and her thick brown legs were crossed at the ankles.

"That shooting scared the living daylights out of me." Aqua said. She was seated on the edge of another sofa chair across the table from Thick Doll, wearing a lacy red Fenty bra and matching boy shorts, sipping on a glass of Casamigos and thumbing through her Instagram news feed. "I mean, I was talking to that boy with the chipped teeth one second, and the next I was ducking under my steering wheel to keep from being shot."

"What can I say? It's K-Town. That's how it goes over there sometimes. Plus, you know, I grew up with Moochie and Mook, went to high school with 'em, too. They're always in some shit." She tilted her head back and toked on the joint she'd fired up a minute ago; it was why she'd put down her book. "Can't really place the blame on them, though. Not this time. Moochie's in the Feds and Mook was at his uncle Ray's party way out in the hundreds when all them people got shot on Monroe."

The potent strain of exotic bud sent Thick Doll into a braying, cringeworthy coughing attack that lasted quite a while. A volley of spittle sprayed from her mouth. Aqua briefly averted her gaze to the mountain of cash on the coffee table between them. Rubber banded stacks of twenties, fifties, and hundreds, the total of it equaling one hundred and twenty-five thousand dollars. She'd given ten grand to Kimmy Kakes, twenty grand to Thick Doll and nothing to Mook and his boys.

For the latter she felt bad.

"Anyways," Thick Doll went on wiping her mouth with the back of her hand, "like I was saying, Mook ain't have shit to do with it this time. A couple of weeks ago, Tails helped his mama set up the bake sale to raise money for his sister's cancer treatment. She raised a few thousand dollars or whatever. I even spent a hundred on one of those nasty ass pumpkin pies. She's lucky it was for a good cause because I was tempted to take that nasty shit right back to her old ass and ask for my refund. But that's neither here nor there. Long story short, word got out that Ms. Miller had all that money and some niggas kicked in her back door the night after the bake sale. Pistol-whipped her until she gave it up. Tails did his little investigation or whatever, and somehow he found out who did it. The Lords over there on Monroe. He went over there with no mask on and shot everybody he caught comin' outta that house."

"They pistol whipped his *mother?*" Aqua asked not disbelieving, really— just trying to get it straight. "Over a few thousand dollars she made from a bake sale?"

"Mmm hm." Thick Doll leaned toward the end table and tapped her joint over the ashtray. Her right tit pooped out of the bathrobe. "I would say I don't blame Tails for what he did, but I hate that he killed that girl. Sabrina was only seventeen and had her whole life ahead of her. It's sad, but I can see why Tails did it. If somebody went and pistol-whipped *my* mama, and took all the money she raised to help *my* sister fight cancer, I prob'ly would've went over there and shot all them people, too."

Aqua shook her head solemnly. She looked down at her phone without really seeing what was showing on its screen. Her eyes kept darting over to Thick Doll, lingering on that exposed tit. It was a pretty titty—such a pretty titty. Looking at it, Aqua's mouth began to water. A part of her felt bad for the unfortunate circumstances Tails and his family were going through, but the sight of Thick Doll's perfect teardrop of a tit had thrown that empathetic part of her to the far back of her brain.

As if to further entice her, Thick Doll set her book down on the end table, picked up the ashtray and her own iPhone, and tiptoed around the coffee table to cozy up next to Aqua. "Here," she said, putting the fat joint to Aqua's lips. "You gotta hit it at least once. I hate being high by myself."

"Right, right." Aqua took a puff so small it was actually a sip. She wanted more—she wanted it *all*— but feared that if she helped herself to a deep lungful, the temptation to suck that beautiful boob right into her mouth would become too overwhelming to resist.

"I wish you would've been told me you had a connect who could just throw bricks at you like that," Thick Doll said, her warm breath tickling Aqua's left ear as she spoke. "I know so many dope boys. Not just here in Chicago, either. All over. My baby daddy used to have me moving bricks some of everywhere."

Aqua looked at her. "I swear, Thick Doll, you—"

"Don't call me that, call me Kari. Only people who don't know the real me call me Thick Doll."

"Well, Kari, I swear, you look so much like Nicole Beharie, it's scary. Same complexion and everything."

"Nicole Be-Who?"

Aqua giggled. "Beharie. She played in that Jackie Robinson movie, she played in American Violet, she played in Miss Juneteenth. Pretty good actress. She ain't all super thick like you, but y'all could definitely pass for sisters. Y'all both so pretty."

Kari gave a little smirk and shrugged her shoulders indifferently. She toked on her joint and blew smoke out her nose, staring straight ahead at a soaring pair of burgundy curtains and the twenty-foot-high set of windows they hung down in front of. Outside, the sky was as dark as Akon's asshole and flecked with stars like dandruff on unclean shoulders. Snowflakes landed against the panes of glass and had just a second or two to be seen in all their crystallized glory before the Burr Ridge mansion's inner heat turned them to falling tears.

"Tomorrow," Kari said, after a long moment, "I'm taking my son to see his daddy's gravesite. It'll be our first visit since the burial, and to be all the way honest with you, I'm not looking forward to it. I'm not looking forward to it at all."

"Yeah?" Aqua was on Princess's Instagram page, jealously browsing through photos and video clips from inside Queen A's exclusive All White party. "You going by yourself, or did you let Prinny talk you into letting a camera crew come along to film it for the show?"

"You know that girl spits more game than a mouthful of poker chips," Kari said and laughed. "Talked me right into it. Said it would be good for ratings, and a memorable moment for my son, and also a good lesson to all the young guys living that street life. Blah, blah, blah." She hit the joint, passed it to Aqua, and held in the smoke so when she spoke again she sounded strangely masculine, like a rapper out to prove to his droves of listeners that he really did smoke blunts and record music simultaneously. "She even talked me into coordinating the gravesite visit with Baby Stone's other dusty, crusty, musty-ass baby mama Shayna, so she can search through that trap house full of kids she got, find the two she had with Baby Stone, and bring them to the cemetery at the same time as me."

Aqua was bubbling over with laughter. She had taken a generous pull on the joint this time around; thick smoke billowed out of her mouth and nose in a wavy gray haze as she fell back next to Kari and laughed like a fool.

"You think I'm bullshittin'?" she said. "I'm really not. That hoe got eighteen kids and countin'. She need to have her own show on TLC. And the bad thing is all her baby daddies are either dead, dead broke, or in prison, so all the kids is scavengers. I made the mistake of taking Lil Jesse over there to see his brother and sister one day. Took him in the backyard with them and the rest of them rascals and let em play while I took a quick thirty-minute nap in my truck, When I went back to get him, my baby was sittin' there butt naked on the back steps, like 'Dang, Mama, they got me'. I ain't bullshittin'."

But she *was* bullshittin'! Aqua could practically see the manure gushing out from Kari's ears. It didn't make the story any less amusing. Aqua was in tears. She mashed out the joint roach in her astray and slid down to the floor, clutching her phone to her gut, howling with laughter. She raised her head and through the blur of tears saw that Kari was laughing right along with her.

"You... are so... *stupid*!" Aqua managed to shout, and when she was finally able to climb back onto the sofa. She downed the remainder of her drink in a single gulp, placed the glass on a coaster on the coffee table, and unfolded the fluffy white and burgundy Hermes quilt she kept draped over the head-end of the sofa. She pulled it up over her and Kari until everything below their chests was cloaked beneath it. "You should've been a comedienne, Kari. Like, for real, for real."

"Mmmm, I make more than enough coins shakin' my ass on that pole every night. That home health care business I started up with my two older sisters is doing good, too. At least this quarter it is."

Kari snatched a furtive glance at her diamond Cartier watch: Aqua saw it from the corner of her eye and assumed it meant Kari was thinking of leaving.

"I got a lap pool in the basement," Aqua said quickly. "An arcade and a bowling alley, too. We can go down there if you want."

"Girl, you sound like a little ass kid tryna keep her best friend from leavin' her house," Kari snickered. "I ain't goin' nowhere. Lil Jesse's at the house with my mama, and you know I ain't got no man."

"Why not?" Aqua turned to look at Kari, seriously wanting to know the answer.

But then her phone rang, and when she looked down she saw that it was the call she'd been waiting on, the sole reason why she hadn't put her phone on Do Not Disturb to keep Fat Perry from calling back-to-fucking back.

"Hold on one second," she said to Kari. Then, she answered the call. "Hello?"

"I'm about to pull in now." It was a woman's voice.

"Okay. It's right inside my front door, in two suitcases. I'm in bed, but I can unlock the door from my phone."

"That's cool. Stay on the phone, though. Just in case the door gets stuck or something."

"I gotchoo," Aqua said, finally putting a name to the voice. It was Tayja, the bad yellow bone who was frequently spotted in the background of Millionaire Markio's selfie videos, the ones that showed him and his entourage laughing it up in the skybox at a Bulls' game or popping bottles on a private jet, or making it rain in strip clubs across the nation. One time, when Markio and his gang essentially took over the VIP Lounge at Queen of Diamonds, Aqua had actually given Tayja a lap dance that lasted through two songs.

That was where Aqua had heard the voice.

She unlocked the front door remotely and then watched from the high-definition camera overlooking the 200-foot driveway that split her neatly manicured lawn in two as a pair of black, presidential looking Escalades cruised in through the wrought iron front gates she'd left open for this very reason.

"We're coming up the driveway now," Tayja said.

"I'm looking at you. The door's open. And please let that man know I want my suitcases returned in the same condition they're in when he gets them. They're Burberry, and my fiancé gifted them to me on my birthday last year."

Tayja issued a tiny yip of a laugh. "I'll have them brought back to you first thing in the morning. No worries." She paused, and for two or three seconds the only sound to be heard from inside her SUV was a soul-stirring Mary J Blige track playing at low volume; then, "Oh my *GOD*. This is one of the most beautiful mansions I've *ever* seen. Markio's house is big like this too, but *this?*" She spoke emphatically, and in wavering tones of astonishment. "This looks like the *White* House! Davion paid for this, didn't he? What did he pay, twenty, twenty-five million?"

Aqua was all smiles up until that last bit about Davion. Even then her sexy smile only faltered a little. She almost came right out with the truth—that she had sold her Streeterville townhouse and drained her checking account of an additional $1.7 million just to secure a 30 year mortgage on the sprawling forty acre Burr Ride property, and that, despite having received a reported $345 million over the span of his NBA career, Davion Carroll hadn't purchased so much as a *spoon* in the house his soon-to-be wife called home— but she knew better than to allow such juicy gossip to fall from her pretty lips. One slip of the tongue, and her business would become The Shade Room's business. So, no, she wasn't going to spill the tea… but she also wasn't going to let Day-Day take the credit for the house she'd bought with her own hard-earned money.

"Twenty-three million," she said, after thinking it over. "And I paid for it myself. It's twenty-two thousand square feet."

"It's a *winner*, is what it is." This was Kari, marveling at those towering burgundy curtains again.

The two SUVs came to a stop in the turnaround. Aqua had pulled her two Rolls-Royces— a cherry red Cullinan and a Phantom of the same color— into the six-car garage to keep them out of the elements, but her Navigator sat directly ahead of where the twin Escalades stood idling, the glaring damage to its right side a cruel reminder of the shooting that had taken place just two hours earlier.

Tayja exited from the rear of the leading Escalade, wearing a furry blue jacket over blue jeans and winter boots, holding an iPhone to her ear and barking orders at two younger men who'd emerged from the second SUV. She led the way toward the front door of the mansion. In they went, and out they came, with Tayja pulling the door closed behind her.

"Okay, we're out," she said watching as the two younger men loaded the suitcases into the back of her SUV. "Boss Man might be at that big party they're having for Alexus at the Castilla, but I'm sure he'll get word to you sometime in the morning."

"Just don't forget about my suitcases. Burberry ain't cheap, you know."

Another yip of laughter from Tayja. "You have my word," she said, and ended the call.

Aqua rested her cheek against Kari's warm shoulder and let out a triumphant sigh. She had just paid Millionaire Markio $400,000 in cash for the twenty kilos of cocaine he'd had delivered to her fourteen hours ago, and now she would wash her hands of the whole terrifying ordeal.

Using her iPhone, she re-engaged the lock on her front door. And when the twin SUVs departed from her driveway, she closed and secured the gates in similar fashion.

"Never again," she swore, talking more to herself than to Kari. "Never a-fucking-gain."

"Yo' scary ass," Kari snickered, shaking her head. Then her gaze settled on the mountain of cash Aqua had stacked upon the coffee table, and she shot another glance at her watch.

Chapter 5

The pain in Kitty Jae's left wrist was almost unbearable, but she did a reasonably decent job at concealing the teeth-clenching agony from her fellow dancers as they changed into their street clothes in the Prime Shift locker room and prepared for tip outs.

"I saw that boy grab you by the arm," Blaire Ketchum, AKA Blicky Nicky, said to Kitty Jae as they stood at their side-by-side lockers, Kitty curling her forefingers into the belt loops of black leather pants to wrestle them up and over the meaty swells of her ass, Blicky pushing one arm into the sleeve of a purple Nike hoodie. "I 'bout ran over there. You know my daddy was a boxer. I'll put the floo-flams on a nigga. Like... *bip-bip-bip*!"

Blicky threw three short jabs at the air between her and her open locker. Her hoodie was only halfway on, hiked up on her golden brown left shoulder and revealing the white belly shirt she wore underneath it and the lavender thong sticking up out of the back of her blue jeans. She was five and half feet tall, slim with a fat bubble of a butt and bee-sting B cups up top. She claimed to be a full-blooded Puerto Rican, but Kitty Jae had never met a Puerto Rican whose Spanish repertoire was limited to just ten or twelve words, and she'd *certainly* never heard of a Puerto Rican with the last name Ketchum.

Kitty Jae winced as she finally got the tight leather pants over her own bubble. Her wrist throbbed ceaselessly. The coke she'd inhaled dulled the ache, but it was still there, a hot, pulsating worm of pain that had wrapped itself around her ulna and refused to leave.

She used only her right hand to push her Gucci belt through the loops in her pants, and she pretty much put on her matching sweatshirt and sneakers the same way, favoring that left wrist. When she was dressed, she checked her iPhone and was relieved to see that her boyfriend of two years and eleven months, Anton Hicks, had texted her four minutes ago saying he was outside waiting.

"Why did he grab you like that anyway?" Blicky asked.

Kitty Jae hoisted her shoulders. "Wanted to know where he could find Princess. I told him I didn't know, but I guess he didn't believe me. So, he grabbed my wrist...." *And squeezed,* is what Kitty Jae wanted to add. Squeezed with those long, bony fingers of his, until her wide, shocked eyes filled with tears, until her legs had come close to collapsing beneath her.

"I just don't understand how Weezy could stand there and watch," said Blicky Nicky. Her voice had taken on a more thoughtful tone. She was standing before the mirror that hung inside the door of her red steel locker, applying a second or third coating of brick-red Fenty lipstick. "You know he saw what happened, right? I saw him look over there when that boy had your arm. Adonis looked too, and he's *security,* for Christ's sake. How is it at all possible that the owner of the fuckin' club and a member of his security team could just stand there and watch while one of us is assaulted? And then to just turn and look away. To turn a fuckin' blind eye. Dirty sons of bitches."

My sentiments exactly, Kitty Jae thought. She'd seen Weezy and Adonis standing there, not more than ten feet away, when she had turned away from Paris, her teary eyes showing clear signs of distress. And for once Blicky Nicky was right: those dirty sons of bitches had looked away. Turned a fuckin' blind eye. They had just led two very important persons into the VIP Lounge, the first being Willie Mosely, a wealthy casino magnate out of New Orleans with a penchant for fine watches and even finer women, and Dr. Rayford Lee McGill, a plastic surgeon who'd quickly become the go-to guy for BBL surgeries during the whole PPP wave. Both men had come with a group of friends and a shitload of cash, and Weezy had been biting into a hot wing while listening as Dr. McGill, who nowadays went by Dr. Chicago, told of some wild yacht party he'd recently thrown somewhere off the Florida coast, but Weezy had locked eyes with Kitty Jae when Paris had his iron grip on her wrist, his magnanimous gaze meeting her frightened, wet-eyed stare.

And yet he'd done nothing. He'd shifted his attention right back to Dr. Chicago and continued their trivial conversation. As if he were not responsible for the safety of the women he employed. As if he wasn't three inches shy of seven feet tall and well over three hundred pounds of mostly rock solid muscle. Adonis was six five, two-sixty and just as solid. The two of them could have wiped the floor with the Hobos. There were placards posted on every wall— spaced every six to eight feet, depending on where you were— that read… THE GOLDEN RULE: NEVER TOUCH THE DANCERS. VIOLATORS WILL BE BANNED FROM THE PREMISES PERMANENTLY. A bit draconian, sure, but it got the point across. Bottom line: the girls were not to be touched. Men had been dumped on their heads for violating that golden rule.

So why hadn't Paris the Hobo suffered a similar fate? Why hadn't Weezy acted to protect Kitty Jae from that skeletal excuse of a man? Why hadn't Adonis picked Paris up by his stick-thin neck and thrown him right down the nearest staircase, punching out any other Hobos who attempted to intervene?

Ruminating over these troubling questions, Kitty Jae sent her body into auto-pilot. All around her the girls were dropping their huge cubes of one-dollar bills into black plastic garbage bags filled with loose bills, so that's what she did. Five lockers down, Cherish Taylor shouldered her purse, pushed her locker shut, turned the dial on her Master Lock, and joined the long queue of Prime Shift dancers who were filing out of their locker room and into the tip-out room further down the hall, so that's what Kitty Jae did.

Almost as if the annoying little bitch had opened a door inside of her head and peered into her brain, Blicky Nicky got in line behind Kitty and said, "You know why I think Weezy ain't do shit? I think the nigga scared. Yup, I said it. He's scared of the Hobos. They've been taking over the Low End, robbin' any and everybody, shootin' and killin' folks, and Weezy don't want no parts of it. *That's* what I think, if you really wanna know."

Kitty Jae brought her chin to rest on her chest, pinched the bridge of her nose, and sighed through her nostrils. *Shut up before you get us both fired*, is what she wanted to say, only she knew that wouldn't work. Blicky would just keep right on bumping her gums, as if no one had ever explained to her the true meaning behind the words 'Shut up'. She had to go another route with the exotic dancer half the other girls called Blabbermouth Blicky. With her, the only real option was to change topics and hope she'd forge along.

"Forget all that," Kitty Jae said, thumbing through the best collection of Halloween photos she'd snapped of OJ on her phone as the line crept forward. "What's up with Princess? Is she thinking of adding any new girls to the cast of *The Real Baddies*?"

"Girl, that's what I've been hoping for this whole time. I asked Big Gabby, but she acts like she don't know shit. I'll tell you like I told that fat bitch: I'm tryna make it from pole to the shows, like Cardi and Meg and all them other stripper bitches. I can rap a lil bit, you know. I got some flow. My daddy was a rapper. Only reason Princess made it is because she got a half-sister whose daddy had a baby with YoungNya, and Bulletface signed YoungNya to Money Bagz

Management, and Alexus is *married* to Bulletface. That's how Princess ended up with the whole MTN deal from the get-go. I swear, I hate a bitch who think her shit don't stank. News flash, Boo-Boo: It does. It really fuckin' does."

"Hmm," Kitty Jae hummed. She picked up her bag of cash and flipped it over her shoulder like Santa with his Christmas sack, partly hoping she'd get lucky and pound Blicky right in the face, but Blicky reared back, weaved to the side, and went right on talking.

"I'm telling you now, if them folks fuck up and let me on that show and *I* get famous, the *first* thing I'm doing is... uhmm." She drifted off, as if there were too many firsts to consider. Then: "I'm buying me a motherfuckin' Rolls-Royce, like the red one Aqua got. Or do she got two of 'em? I think she do. A truck and a car. I seen 'em on the show, parked out in front of that big-ass mansion she got. I bet she got at *least* fifty million dollars in the bank."

Kitty Jae snorted. "Not hardly. Kimmy Kakes told me how much they make on that show. It's a little over thirty thousand per episode, and there are ten episodes per season, so they end up with about three hundred grand before taxes."

"I can sleep with that." Blicky nodded wishfully.

"You'd make a lot more off the publicity. Especially if you had something to sell, some kinda product. Being on TV puts more eyes on you. That's the kind of influencer all the business owners look for. I overheard Shmoney Rose telling somebody over the phone how she had just made fifty grand for some kinda promo deal. All she gotta do is post a pic of herself on IG wearing some kinda knee-high socks and tag the business page, and the money's hers."

Blicky shrugged. "I still say Aqua's rollin' in it. She's the only one engaged to an NBA player. He probably gave her twenty million just on GP." Her phone rang. She looked at it, held up a forefinger to Kitty Jae, and answered the call in the most ratchet, obnoxiously loud voice she could convoke.

Like how Regina Hall's character in *Scary Movie* had answered her phone in the theater. *Hello* came out *how-low*.

"Kitty Jae didn't mind the interruption. Their conversation would have ended seconds later anyway, because the line moved up four or five more feet, and they turned and stepped through the open doorway of the tip-out room.

The room was big and square, with plain white walls and gray stone flooring, very utilitarian. Three long wooden fold-out tables positioned in a U-formation, stood in the middle of the floor. The girls only stopped and lifted their cash-filled bags onto the side tables to take out the dollars they were required to pay the four men and women who stood near the back table.

Those four men and women were Big Gabby, the House Mom, to whom each of the girls had to pay twenty-five dollars at the end of every shift; DJ Rackz Up, a short, flashy-dressing disc jockey with big ears, dark skin and a seemingly endless supply of White Sox fitted caps, received five dollars from each girl for his skills on the ones and twos; Nyomi Banxxx, a veteran porn star with eyes like a feline and skin like a Hershey's chocolate bar fresh out of the wrapper had landed the role as this week's host and would receive ten bucks from each dancer for her services; and Weezy, who represented the House, was owed five dollars from every twenty dollar lap dance given, twenty for every fifty dollar private dance, and (under the table, of course) twenty percent of the proceeds the quasi-prostitutes in the bunch had made for the exchange of sexual favors in the private rooms upstairs.

Relegating the task of collecting his share to Big Gabby, who piled it neatly on the table beside her own share, Weezy spent his time shooting the shit with the DJ, hugging the girls and bidding them goodnight in between words. He stopped to stare at Kitty Jae when he saw her but that didn't necessarily portend anything sinister. She was a bad bitch.

Men stared at her all the time. Only this room was literally *teeming* with bad bitches, and in Kitty Jae's experience, when men were faced with a room full of beautiful women, their eyes tended to dart around, like the wide eyes of a cock-starved debutante who has just begun her journey down an aisle of dildos at her local sex shop.

Kitty Jae lowered her gaze against the heavy burden of the big man's stare and lifted her bag onto the table. She'd made out nicely for a Thursday night. Thanks in large part to Willie Mosely, who'd handed over four grand for a shot of anal in Blue Room #4. His dick had been long and thick in his extra-large condom, but the only real pain Kitty remembered feeling during their fifteen-minute romp was the low throb in her wrist. Never one to complain, she'd gone down to her forearms on the L-shaped Blue Room sofa, keeping her fat ass in the air and allowing the forty something Mr. Willie Mosely to ream her tight little butthole to completion. Much to Willie's credit he'd given Kitty Jae the orgasm she'd been yearning for all night. Making her pussy drip-drip-drip down onto the sofa. When he asked for her personal phone number afterward, she'd given it to him, urging him to only text the number and never to call unless she gave him the okay.

"Did you get a look at the clean-ass Bentley Weezy pulled up in?" Blicky Nicky asked as she dropped her bag next to Kitty's. She didn't wait for an answer; she rarely ever did. "It's called a *Batur*. Ever heard of that?" Again, no wait. "Sounds like a sneeze or a spit, don't it? *Batur.* I'll tell you what, though, that motherfucker sure don't *look* like a sneeze. Least not one I ever seen. It's a two-door, like a dark purple, and it only got the two seats in the front. You know I had to Google it. Starting price is two *million.* He let me sit next to him in that passenger seat, I'll *Batur* all over dat *dick.* You hear me?"

The giggle that burst from Kitty Jae's mouth was sudden and completely involuntary. Blicky Nicky sometimes had that effect on people. However, in spite of the humorous moment, Kitty Jae could not help but to think of the words she'd heard from the old man on her porch five months ago. *Give me a ring the next time Weezy shows his face in that club he owns over there on 73rd and Cottage, and let me know what kind of car he's driving. You do that and the money's all yours.*

Five hundred thousand dollars.

More than enough cash to repay that business loan and at least get a good start on the production of her very first horror film. She had already written the screenplay. It would require some rewriting here and there, and maybe a slight restructuring of the storyline, but the plot itself was guaranteed to elicit some soul piercing screams from the viewers, and the climax was what real nightmares were made of. Upon its release, the film would undoubtedly be hailed a… what was the word all those movie critics were fond of using?

"A blockbuster," Kitty Jae said.

"Bitch, what?" Blicky Nicky scrunched her face.

"Nothing."

With the cash they owed out in hand, they continued on. Kitty Jae, feeling particularly charitable with all the cash she had in her bag, gave a twenty to both the DJ and Host, gave Big Gabby a fifty, and was in the process of counting out the cash she owed Weezy when he came over and slipped an arm around her shoulders. His suit looked very expensive, and he smelled very deserving of wearing it, as if he'd showered and dressed not even thirty minutes ago.

"Go on and put that lil paper back in your bag," he said. His mouth was close to her ear. His breath drifted around to her nose and brought with it the fragrant scent of Cognac.

He didn't have to tell her twice. She'd already tied her black plastic Glad bag in a knot, so she slipped the hundreds— crisp new Benjamins from the money Willie

Mosely had paid her— into her Gucci purse, and when Big Gabby gave her a look, she pointed at Weezy.

"I got this," he said, his lips approximating a smile. "Kitty, let me talk to you for a minute."

Kitty Jae's reluctance could not have been more apparent, and her disdain was even more evident, as she allowed Weezy to take her by the elbow and move away from the tables. She looked at him from the corner of her eye, too pissed to even look at him straight-on. He must have glimpsed a flicker of the true hellfire she felt burning hot behind her eyes, because all of a sudden he went from guiding her over to the back wall to preceding her out into the hallway and out through the heavy blue steel door that opened into the rear parking lot.

A blue steel railing bordered the concrete walkway just outside the door. Kitty Jae sucked in a lungful of cold air and watched it fog out in front of her on the exhale, leaning her hip against the gelid steel pipe of the railing and watching as several other Prime Shift girls, escorted by a motley clan of boyfriends and bouncers, hurried off toward their vehicles. Johnny "Jigga Man" Stewart, a tall, charcoal black bouncer with a distinctive limp, stood guard at the end of the walkway, smoking a cigarette as the light snowfall created shimmery white specks all over his loose-fitting black hoodie.

Parked in the reserved slot directly in front of Jigga was a sleek purple Bentley Batur.

"Nice, ain't it?" Weezy said, following her gaze. "I just paid two-point-two million for that coupe right there. The most expensive production Bentley ever made, and they only made eighteen of 'em. That motherfucker goes sixty in three point three seconds and maxes out at two oh-nine. Ike Turner couldn't beat that bitch."

Kitty Jae had already turned away from the cute little two-seater that had clearly captured all of Weezy's heart. Her deeply intelligent eyes moved eight parking spaces to her left, where her black-on-black G Wagon sat idling like an ebony Goliath. Then she turned back to Weezy. She had to tilt her head back to look up at him.

"Well, I guess I'm *Tina* Turner." She said smartly. "R-E-S-P-E-C-T, find out what it means to me, because I didn't feel respected at all in that VIP Lounge tonight."

"Ha haaaa!" Weezy laughed, his unfortunately shaped bald head falling back on brawny shoulders, his wide-open mouth catching a dozen or more snowflakes before his head came back down to look at her. "See now, that – that was a good one. That was a good one."

"It wasn't a joke."

"Nah, I know, I know, I know. And that's my bad. Had a few shots up there in my office, got me feelin' myself a lil bit. But listen." Weezy brought his right hand up to his mouth and balled it into a loose fist to clear his throat in a respectable fashion. Oddly though, the fingers couldn't quite fold over; they were wrinkled and sallow, more gray than brown, the fingers of a zombie who'd been walking around dead for eight days and eight nights. "I sincerely apologize for what happened up—"

"Why didn't you help me?" Kitty Jae interjected. She had her arms folded over her chest, gripping her heavy bag of money in one hand like an overweight chicken with its neck wrung. "Were you scared? Hm? You and big, bad Adonis afraid of the Hobos? Was that it? Because that's sure in the fuck how it seemed to me."

Weezy's humorous smile became a serious scowl very suddenly. In that same moment Kitty Jae realized that, whether happy or angry, Weezy was an exceptionally ugly man.

"I ain't scared of nobody," he said and nothing else.

Kitty could tell by the timbre of his voice and glare in his eyes that he felt he was being intimidating. She was unmoved. The door behind him swung open and slammed shut as Blicky Nicky and another Prime Shift dancer called

Sasha the Stallion departed the building. Sasha went marching toward her sky blue Rolls-Royce Ghost, the only thing she had to show for her fleeting romance with MBM's Young Meach, but Blicky stopped to hug and chat with Jigga… and likely to eavesdrop on Kitty and Weezy's discussion.

All this Kitty saw in her periphery; she and Weezy were currently engaged in a staring war, and she was determined not to lose.

"Don't ever disrespect me like that again," he said after some time. "God ain't made a nigga who can scare Roy Sullivan."

"How is it that you're the one who feels disrespected when I'm the one who almost got my wrist broken?"

"They're mad. You gotta understand that. A nigga Princess used to fuck with shot the dog shit outta Paris and one of the other Hobos. And then, when they sent two of their shorties over there to kill that nigga, Princess killed both of them boys. MCG and Snake. Keytron Douglas and Donte Edgebrook. They were Gutterville Mickey Cobras, but they were related to Bowlegs, so you might as well say they were honorary Hobos, too."

"What that go to do with me?"

"Will you just listen? Damn," Weezy said, his tone replete with exasperation. "Like I was sayin', they're mad as fuck right now. Grind, the nigga who shot Paris and the other Hobo, just got released from jail sometime yesterday. Princess done got all rich and famous off a show she made about some bad bitches who dance right here at Queen of Diamonds, and all night she's been on Instagram, partying with Queen A and Bey and all the rest of the letters in the celebrity alphabet, while Paris sat in there all shot up, tryna figure out how to even the score."

"Am I missing something here?" Kitty's hands were starting to get cold. Between her two eyes, she could see that her nose had become a ruddier shade of red.

"What you're missing is this," Weezy said, and this time when the big steel door swung open behind him, he reached back and caught it, a clear sign that their conversation was coming to an end. "Princess's new boyfriend is from over your way, am I right?" He was like Blicky Nicky, not even allowing time for an answer. "He grew up around the same niggas you grew up around. Paris knew that. That's why he grabbed you. Had I intervened and thrown him out of my club, I would've ended up on Millionaire Markio's side of the beef, and that's the side I'm no longer on. Now if he would've hit you or choked you, something like that, I'd have done something. But he only grabbed your wrist. That ain't worth killing somebody over, and believe me, that's what it would've came to."

Kitty Jae had heard enough; the roll of her eyes said as much. She stormed off down the walkway, moving fast, not looking back. Blicky Nicky fell in step beside her and was asking if everything was good when Weezy shouted from the open doorway.

"That nigga Markio," he said, "his old ass uncle cut my hand off! Fuck him and Princess! If I wasn't makin' no money off that bitch, she'd be dead right along with the nigga!"

"I'll be sure to deliver that message," Kitty Jae muttered, lifting her phone to send out a text to an old friend. Emphasis on the *old*.

Chapter 6

Kari initiated the sexual contact Aqua so obviously wanted with a soft kiss to the corner of her pretty mouth, and Aqua sat straight up and turned into the kiss, taking Kari's face in her small, delicate hands and reciprocating with a bombardment of soft-lipped kisses that were much more passionate in nature.

The time on Kari's iced-out watch was 2:37. At this time of morning Queen of Diamonds was preparing to close for the night. The parking lot was rapidly emptying, the Prime Shift girls were tipping out and leaving out the back door four figures richer than they were when they tipped in, and Big Gabby was taking all the cash the club had pulled in from door fees, food and liquors sales, and tip-outs up to Weezy's office, where it would languish in a floor safe until she transported it to the bank around noon. Kari knew that routine like she knew all of the avenues between Pulaski and Cicero on Chicago's west side.

It was a good thing she liked Weezy; otherwise, she'd have had big Gabby robbed a long while ago.

She closed her arms around Aqua's waist as the young woman mounted her beneath the Hermes blanket. She moved her head back and to the side, offering up her neck as if she were some helpless white woman in a vampire romance, and Aqua's open mouth fell upon her carotid artery as if she intended to sink her teeth in and suck out every last drop of blood.

No teeth entered the equation, but there certainly was a lot of sucking. Licking and kissing, too. Up the left side of Kari's next to her left ear and behind it— that forbidden area of skin Kari considered her *spot*, usually elongating the word for emphasis— then back down to her neck and down a bit more, throwing open the thick black robe to latch onto that gorgeous tit she'd had her eye on twenty minutes prior. Kari had seen the stare. That stare was the reason she abandoned her Zane book to sashay across the capacious ballroom and cozy up next to Aqua to begin with.

Aqua flickered her tongue across Kari's perfect brown nipple. Kari gasped shakily and, underneath the comforter, smacked both hands onto Aqua's fat yellow ass. The smack elicited a carnal moan from Aqua. The moan expelled a warm breath of air onto the nipple she had her full pink lips wrapped around, forcing Kari to arch her back and issue a falsetto of her own sexy little moans.

"You makin' me wet." Kari whined.

"That's a good thing," Aqua replied, going lower, her head disappearing beneath the blanket. "I was just starting to get thirsty."

Oddly enough, Karionna Patrice Washington did not consider herself bisexual, and she most certainly was not gay. She loved dick like Bobby Brown had loved Whitney Houston, like P Diddy had loved Cassie Ventura— a love hate relationship but a love all the same. The only other woman she'd ever been sexually intimate with was Michelle "Big Mike" Spears, the gorilla she'd found herself bunked up with at Cook County Jail in the summer of 2020. Kari had been alone in the jail cell for nineteen days, facing attempted murder charges for allegedly shooting Shayna Hartwell, the mother of her baby daddy's other two children, twice in the gut with a nine millimeter pistol, when suddenly the cell door buzzed open and in walked Big Mike— a six foot five, three hundred pound beast of masculinity with cornrows, one droopy eye, and a mirthy little grin that stayed turned on when she was sleeping.

S'up, she'd said upon entering the cell.

Hey, Kari had replied in the most sexually suggestive tone of voice she could muster up— not because she had found anything attractive about the towering ape, but because she'd secreted a tied-off sandwich bag containing thirty four capsules of Molly inside her rectum when the police pulled her over nineteen days earlier and she had swallowed one with the lukewarm coffee that had come with her breakfast tray not even thirty minutes prior to Big Mike's arrival. She'd been lying back on the top bunk with her hands behind her head and her eyes on the ceiling, feeling the vaginal juices started to soak through her cheap cotton jail panties and contemplating masturbation as she visualized Kevin Hart keeling between her parted thighs, leaning in over her and informing her that she was going to learn what a big dick looked like that particular day, when big Mike came in holding a mesh bag filled with jail issued clothing, bedding and off-brand hygiene products under one pillar sized arm and a cold tray of breakfast in her other hand.

Less than an hour later, Kari had ditched her undies and the multi-stained pants of her jail uniform, sat with her naked legs swinging over the side of her bunk, and allowed Big Mike to push them up and go to town.

Her and Big Mike's introduction had transpired at a time when she was high, horny and in serious need of sexual release. She'd seen Big Mike as a temporary means of an end, and she'd used her for that very purpose.

Now she was using Aqua—not because she was aroused and in dire need of relief, but for a much better reason– and she didn't feel bad about it at all.

Kari's iPhone lay face-up beside the ashtray she'd set on the ebony table next to Aqua's sofa chair. She reached over and grabbed it… just as Aqua's tongue tapped the sensitive nub of her clitoris. She inhaled nasally, arching her back, anxiously awaiting the next titillating tap, even as Aqua began planting gentle kisses along her inner thigh. *Just eat my fucking pussy!* Kari's brain screamed but that was merely the nymph in her talking, that primal voice that had compelled her to let a gargantuan ogre have its way with her in county lockup. Then the quieter, calmer, and wiser thought came through loud and clear: *Send out the text, Kari, before she looks up and figures out what you're doing.*

The text message was already composed. She'd typed it up while she was grazing over the bookshelves, trying to decide which novelist she wanted to spend her time with most: Walter Mosely, JaQuavis Coleman, Donald Goines, Latonya West or Zane. There were a hundred other authors on the shelves, all of them African American bestsellers, but Kari had settled on just the five, and she'd taken her time doing it— hoping that whoever Aqua's plug was sending to collect the money would hurry up and get there so she could finally hit SEND on the text.

Kari turned on her phone screen and thumbed her way to the message. *It's a go*, it read. Licking her lips as Aqua's long, pink tongue moved slowly up the slit of her swollen vagina petals, Kari began typing out one more sentence.

"You must eat a lot of fruit," Aqua said from down yonder.

"Why you say that?"

"Because you taste good. The sugar in the fruit gives your pussy a sweet taste."

"Well, it must be all the Starbursts and Now and Laters I eat, because I ain't had no fruit in God knows—"

Kari's words came to an abrupt halt as Aqua's soft lips closed around her clitoris. She filled her lungs with air. Her eyeballs rolled upward and her eyelids fluttered spasmodically as Aqua's flicking tongue became like a light heavyweight boxer's gloved fists hammering away at a speed bag, knocking her engorged clit back and forth with an accuracy that in the moment seemed almost superhuman.

Her head fell back and her mouth fell open. Shakily, she sucked in a breath without ever having to exhale the last one, swelling her lungs to capacity. When she finally did exhale, it all came out of her in one great whoosh, its accomplice a moaning yelp of such high pitch it might have made Mariah Carey stand and bow, had she heard it.

Meanwhile, Aqua went on sucking and licking, treating the clitoris in her mouth like a Jolly Rancher candy she was determine to suck on until there was nothing left to suck. She inserted a middle finger almost to the third knuckle and probed around for Kari's G-spot, and when that proved futile she added a second finger, and half a minute later, a *third*.

This time an entire series of Carey-worthy notes escaped Kari's gaping mouth. Her eyes bulged in their sockets. The patchwork blanket slid sideways off Aqua's back and crumpled to the floor just in time to provide padding for the iPhone that slipped from Kari's twitching fingers.

"Oh shit," Kari said, an expletive that bore two meanings. The first was a reaction to Aqua's unrelenting oral ministrations. The second was in reaction to her own stupidity; she'd just dropped her phone after only having typed two words to the extra sentence she intended to add "Oh shit," she repeated. "I dropped my... I dropped my, my, my... *PHONE!*"

The last words came out in a jarring scream. She was coming and *O Magazine* had nothing on the big 'O' she was experiencing. Eyes wide, her mouth stretched even wider, she balled handfuls of her borrowed robe in her fists and held on tight as her body succumbed to the all-encompassing tremors that always came chasing after her orgasm, like Wile E. Coyote after Road Runner. She let loose another of those high, shrill cries. Her eyes rolled upward again, as if attempting to study the underside of her brain. And when they came down from snooping she saw that Aqua had moved back a little and was massaging her softening clitoris in slow, sensuous circles.

"Ooouu, look at thaaatt." Aqua said dreamily. "It's trickling down over your bootyhole. Let me get some'a that before you soak my damn couch."

Aqua lowered her head rather quickly and began slurping up the escaping juices, and when she was done her attention shifted to Kari's butthole. Aqua was renowned for her long tongue, and now she put it to use, poking and prodding at Kari's virgin-tight sphincter until she got it loose enough to slither in deeper.

Once the tremors and their immediate aftershocks had fully subsided, Kari managed to reach down beside the sofa and recover her phone. She typed in one more word to the sentence she'd added and hit SEND.

The message read: *It's a go. Two black Escalades.*

Two short sentences, but they were more than enough.

The GPS tracking device Kari had slipped into one of Aqua's beloved Burberry suitcases would do the rest.

Chapter 7

"I don't see how you can drink that stuff every day," the thickly proportioned Kamari White said.

Millionaire Markio cracked a smile while simultaneously cracking the seal on a fresh pint of Wockhardt promethazine with codeine syrup. Out of the corner of his eye, he captured a glimpse of Kamari as she folded her arms across her buxom chest and leaned her voluminously sloping hip against the gray marble countertop six feet to the left of him. Her skin complexion was like Hershey's chocolate syrup squeezed right out of the bottle. She had long dark hair that was braided in narrow cornrows on one side of her scalp and spilled down the other side in radiant curls— as if she had made it halfway through a hairdressing session before revealing to the stylist that she didn't have the money to pay for the appointment. Her off-white Dior sweater was so incongruously baggy that it covered the spandex shorts she wore beneath it, exposing her long, meaty legs in a way that made her appear half naked.

In effort to keep his mind and eyes off the mesmerizing sight of his girlfriend's twenty-one-year old sister, he forced himself to focus on the thirst-quenching task at hand, fixing himself a cup of Lean, his favorite beverage of choice.

Standing before him on the counter were two Styrofoam cups, one stacked inside the other, and a two-liter container of Sprite, still cold from the stainless-steel fridge he'd just taken it from.

Carefully, he poured exactly four ounces of syrup into the Styrofoam, which he'd already filled to the halfway mark with Sprite. He dropped five ice cubes into the fizzing narcotic beverage, picked up the cup and stirred the contents with a few rotations of his wrist.

"Ain't nothin' wrong with a lil sip-sip. I didn't criticize you and Princess for drinking all that Casamigos on your birthday," Markio said, finally replying to Kamari's statement.

"Yeah, but that's different," she argued. "Everybody drinks alcohol. It lightens the mood, brings joy and laughter during the darkest of times. That shit you're drinking is a *drug*."

"Ethanol is a drug, too." Markio returned his ingredients to their assigned shelves in the refrigerator. Then he took a small sip from his cup, nodded his head appreciatively, and offered the cup to Kamari.

She demurred, scrunching her sexy round face in disgust. "Not in a million years. I'll keep on drinkin' my ethanol, thank you very much." She was a native Chicagoan, but a bit of the Arkansas drawl had attached itself to her accent during her college years down in Pine Bluff. It sounded sweet coming from her.

Mario took a noisy slurp from his cup, collected his two iPhones from the countertop, and started out of the enormous second-floor kitchen. Kamari flicked off the light switch and followed him out into the wide, dark hallway, padding along behind him on bare feet that were warmed by the heated marble floor.

They were at the House of Lords, the 25,000 square foot Lincoln Park mansion Markio had recently purchased from one of Alexus Costilla-King's billionaire associates. He'd paid a little over $31 million for the property with all the opulent furnishing included. The previous owner, an eccentric Italian shoe designer name Kitanya Pullizzi, had left behind a priceless collection of artwork, fifteenth century masterpieces that graced the walls in every bedroom and hallway, including the one he and Kamari were now traipsing through— he in his white and gray Louis Vuitton sweatpants and white leather Louis flip flops, she in her oversized sweater.

CHING-CHING... CHING-CHING-CHING... CHING-CHING...

The sounds of the seven diamond necklaces and heavy diamond pendants that hung from Millionaire Markio's neck was like metal clashing against metal. He'd paid more than a million dollars for the jewelry. The diamond-encrusted Rolex Sky Dweller he wore on his right wrist had cost him another hundred and fifty grand. The film adaptation to his New York Times best-selling novel, *The Bird Man*, had grossed $332 million, and he'd pocketed a substantial sum of that money, but when it was all said and done he was just another gang member who'd made it out of the slums. There was Oscar buzz surrounding his debut film, and when award season rolled around he would don his suit and tie and walk the red carpet with the rest of Hollywood's elite, but he didn't believe he'd ever truly be comfortable in their presence. Not without his gang members somewhere nearby. Sure, he was a critically acclaimed urban fiction novelist, but he was more Donald Goines than Carl Webber, so tied to the streets that he might end up shot dead inside his glorious Lincoln Park mansion if he wasn't careful.

And yet he still loved the streets.

He was a high-ranking member of the Traveling Vice Lords, a fact that all the money and fame in the world couldn't change. Most of his tattoos — from the huge ALMIGHTY inked across his upper back in cursive lettering to the even larger CUP GANG tatted across his incipient beer belly—perhaps codeine belly was a more accurate choice of wording—were gang related. He wore Louis Vuitton because of its overlapping LV logo for Vice Lord, and he'd christened his home the *House of Lords* because, aside from a close relative and a select few associates, Vice Lords were the only people he allowed inside the walls of his four-story gray stone palace.

In all honesty, Markio Earl loved his gang more than he loved any of the centuries-old Renaissance paintings that hung on the walls in the many rooms and Art Deco inspired hallways inside the House of Lords.

"Speaking of drinking," Kamari said in a near whisper as she pulled up alongside him. "Prinny is *slapped* right now. She called me a few minutes ago. I could hardly understand anything she said. She's drunk as I don't know what."

Markio shook his head, ground his teeth together, and fought back an indignant sneer. "She be tweakin' hard as hell," he said. In his Chicago accent, *hard* came out *hahd*. "I knew I should've went to that party. My gut told me to go too."

"Your gut should've told you to do about fifty sit-ups."

Markio looked over and up and let that sneer out of its cage. Kamari showed a beatific smile. It seemed like she'd grown another inch or so in the last six months. She was maybe six-three. Markio, like Princess, was much shorter, like Leonid in that book series by Walter Mosely, or Lil Wayne, the New Orleans rap god whose lyrical genius had inspired Markio's literary career from the beginning. And perhaps, subconsciously, the rapper had even influenced Markio's propensity for sipping Lean.

It never occurred to him that he could have actually met Wayne in person had he gone to Alexus's all-white affair. He was about two-thirds of the way finished writing the screenplay to *The Bird Man's* highly anticipated sequel, and he was determined to complete it before the Thanksgiving holiday.

Halfway down the hallway, he made a left turn into his study, the massive room where he did all his writing. It was a grand hall of an office, the very picture of opulence. Thick crimson carpet ran between gold veined white marble walls upon which hung Renaissance masterpieces illuminated from the ceiling by spotlights.

Eight steps into the room he and Kamari passed the fully stocked Egyptian mahogany bar that was built into the wall on the right. Kamari stopped to peruse the many bottles of liquor, while Markio continued on.

Twenty-nine more steps across carpeting that felt like goose down pillows underfoot and Markio arrived at his desk. Also carved from Egyptian mahogany, the desk was nearly as wide as a dining table, and standing behind it like a jet black specter was a comfortable leather swivel chair that was large enough to seat a giant.

Settling into the bovine upholstery, Markio rolled forward and typed in the password to gain access to his Apple computer. First he spent a moment studying the images from his indoor home security cameras, not to catch anyone in the act of wrongdoing but to make sure his two-year-old son, Markio Earl, Jr., and Prinny's five-year-old daughter Vee were sleeping soundly in their bedroom two doors down. They were.

"No need in sending anybody to pick Prinny up." Kamari said, crossing the floor to Markio's desk and taking a seat in one of the two seventeenth century French chairs that stood before it. "Alexus has a driver bringing her home. I think it might be Bojo, that cocky ass Mexican. The one who's always standing behind Alexus when the TMZ cameras catch her out in Hollywood."

"She'll be good." Markio muttered vacantly. He was looking in on the ten-man dice game that was taking place in the heated comfort of the twenty-car garage.

The men were huddled behind Markio's snow white Lamborghini Aventador, a few of them kneeling, a few others bent forward, all of them holding piles of cash and passing around blunts of Raspberry Gelato, the most potent strain of high-grade bud on the market. Among them were Kay and Buck, two of Markio's older cousins: Cocky Lord,

Baby James, Big Luke, Gucci Ball, Bam, Big Keanan, Baby Lord, and Jahlil.

All ten of them were Traveling Vice Lords.

"You don't sound all that concerned," Kamari opined.

Markio exited the camera system and turned his attention to Kamari just as she was lifting her thick legs on the chair, offering him a fleeting glimpse of her tiny black yoga shorts.

"What?"

"You heard me. You don't sound all that concerned. My sister is drunk in the backseat of some stranger's car, so out of it that she could hardly even put two sentences together, and the only thing you can say is 'She'll be good'?"

Markio sipped. "Mind your business."

"She is *my* business. We came out the same womb. Psshhh. It's a good thing you ain't my man. I would've dumped your ass a looongg time ago." Kamari spoke brusquely, but that beatific smile was present all the while, lit from the glowing screen of the smartphone she'd eased out of the sleeve of her oversized sweater. She was toying with him like she always did. "A good, nice boyfriend would've *immediately* called his girl to make sure she was okay, to make sure she wasn't being taken advantage of by the seven-foot Mexican she has in the car with her."

"I'm a Vice Lord," Markio said, "not a *nice* Lord. And I can't focus on what my girl got goin' on because right now I got a seven-foot *African* sitting in my office at two forty-five in the morning *buggin'* me."

"Oh, shut up, shortstop." Her imitation eyelashes fluttered rapidly, and that annoying yet attractive smile of hers widened. "I ain't no seven-foot nothin'. I'm six two… and three quarters."

"What do you want?"

"What do I want? Let's see, uhmm… Well, for starters, I want a role in your next movie."

"Done. You'll play a crackhead prostitute who sucks dick for nickels. Now what else?"

Kamari cracked up laughing, tossing her head back, slapping her knee. Markio tried suppressing his own laughter and failed, so the two of them laughed together for a time, like two chaste in-laws over a hand of spades— only there was nothing chaste about the palpable tension between Kamari and him.

"I hate you," she said, meaning the opposite.

"Why you got on that big ass sweater?"

"It was my daddy's."

Lowering her head, Kamari lifted the diamond encircled pendant that hung from her thin gold necklace and stared at it. Markio stared too. The photo in the pendant showed a smirking Lejon White, an infamous Gangster Disciple from the south side of Chicago who'd gone by the name Grizzy.

"He got killed in my neighborhood," Markio said somberly.

"I know. On Kedzie, right across from that convenience store. Nya shot back and killed one of them, but the damage was already done. My daddy died in the backseat of his Rolls-Royce."

"He gave'em hell before he went, though. Grizzy and Nya— they were like Bonnie and Clyde, from what I hear. And *after* he died…" Markio shook his head and sipped. The fat diamond ring on his pinkie finger clicked against the wood of his desk when he put his cup back down. "Nya really went nuts then. They say she was the one who killed Bryce and his cousin Jabar over there on Washington and Kostner. Then she caught Red Rum on Chicago Avenue and Central and whacked him on his front porch. And you know what's crazy? She did all that shit after she had already signed her record deal with MBM. That's why I keep shorty on my playlist. She with the shits like baby diapers."

Kamari had become maudlin at the talk of her deceased father, her smile dimming from a thousand watts to somewhere around four hundred, her eyes growing misty with tears, but the wattage of her gorgeous smile increased when Markio finished speaking.

She snorted a laugh, dried her eyes with the sleeve of her sweater, and said, "That's funny. 'With the shits like baby diapers.' I never heard that one before."

"I never said that one before."

"Shut *up*. You ain't no originator." She sniffled, regarded him with a sneer that was more comical than contemptuous, then started typing something on her phone.

Markio snatched a glance at the crotch of Kamari's skintight yoga shorts before turning to his computer to access the Microsoft Word document that contained his screenplay he'd been working on since late September, and once he had it up on the screen, he chanced a second glance. Then a third, fourth, and fifth. She had a camel toe that to Markio looked like a double cheeseburger standing sideways.

"How many people you done killed?" Kamari asked out of nowhere. Her phone disappeared back into the sleeve of her sweater. "All bullshit aside. Give me a number."

"Zero." Markio lied, and without a moment's hesitation.

Her juicy lips moved skeptically aside. "You do know I looked you up when you started dating my sister, right? I read those interviews you did with XXL and Time magazines too. You did fifteen years for a murder that happened somewhere in... I don't remember the city, but I know it's in Indiana, and that it ain't too far from here."

Markio pushed out his lower lip and didn't speak. Memories of arrests from long ago surfaced in his mind. White men built like soldiers slapping handcuffs on his wrists and reciting the ominous Miranda rights they all seemed to know so well. *You have the right to remain silent. Anything you say can and will be used against you in a court of law. You have the right to an attorney....* Blah, blah, blah. They were better off just saying *Mister Negro, your ass is in three-foot-high grass, and my name is John Deere.*

"Okay, okay," Kamari said, capitulating. "I get why you won't answer that one. I tweaked on that one. What about, uhmm, like the money you've made in the streets? I overheard my daddy talkin' about you with some of his cousins. They had just bought two bricks of coke from Bam. You know Bam and Big Worm were his connects back in the day— and I heard my daddy say that you were, like, the plug of all plugs, that Bam started copping from you after his brother Worm got killed. That true?"

"You ask a lot of incriminating questions."

Kamari sucked her teeth, repositioning her legs in the chair. "You get on my last nerve," she mumbled, producing her phone again. "Fuckin' jerk."

Markio shrugged indifferently and picked up the iPhone he used to manage and oversee the numerous branches of his drug empire. The phone was registered in a bogus name, the camera lenses were tapped over, and the geolocation was switched off. Markio had never made a call from the phone; he only sent and received text messages via What's App, coded messages that only he and his crew would understand.

He had only one new message. It was from Tayja, and the message consisted of just four thumbs down emojis, which actually meant thumbs-up. A confirmation that she had completed all four cash pickups and was now enroute to the stash house to put it all away until he said otherwise.

$800,000 from the forty kilos he'd sold to Dion Wiliams and his boy Lil Daryl out of Indianapolis, Indiana; $400,000 from the twenty bricks he'd been reluctant to front to Aqua; and $200,000 apiece from Bam and Jahlil, both of whom had purchased a hundred pounds of Raspberry Gelato for the one-time price of $2,000 a pound.

$1.6 million on a snow-drizzled night in November.

If smiling from ear to ear was a literal possibility, Markio would have done it at that very moment.

He pulled open his top desk drawer, flipped up the lid of a gold-plated cigar box that held forty-two pre-rolled blunts of Raspberry Gelato, and lit one with diamond encrusted Zippo he'd gotten as a gift from Blake and Alexus last Christmas. With the overstuffed blunt wedged between the first two fingers of his right hand and his Styrofoam cups gripped firmly in his left, he sat back in his chair and blew a stream of thick gray smoke as hard as he could in Kamari's direction.

"Bitch," he said, beaming.

Kamari looked up to glare at him and then did an excited double take. "Ooooouuu, is that, that Raspberry? Let me hit that."

"Bye, Felicia."

"You got me fucked up, Markio." She stood up and walked around his desk, reaching for his blunt. When he moved it out of her reach, she turned her huge ass to him and plopped it down onto his lap, taking hold of the armrests to keep him trapped beneath her.

As if he or any man with a healthy appetite of the opposite sex would have made any sort of significant attempt at slipping from beneath all the ass that she possessed.

"Get the fuck off me, maan," he said, not meaning it at all. She reached for the blunt with both hands, the chair spun ninety degrees to the right, and Markio was able to set his cup on the desk and slip his right hand behind Kamari's back, switching the blunt over to his left hand while laughing at her failed endeavor. "You ain't strong enough, lil lady. I got grown man strength. Did a thousand push-ups almost every day for fifteen years in prison."

"Let me hit the goddamn blunt." Kamari said, in wavering tones of resignation.

"Say please."

She sucked her teeth, folding her arms across her chest and pouting like the kid she'd been not all that long ago.

"Say please," Markio repeated.

The phone he used to conduct legitimate business and to socialize with his family and friends buzzed and lit up on the table. *Probably a text from an ex,* Markio thought, knowing that the screen of his phone only turned on from phone calls, text messages, and notifications from his home security app.

"Please," Kamari said finally, and nothing more.

Markio gave her the blunt. She puffed on it and stayed put, shifting around a bit as his dick grew hard in his sweats. He placed a hand on her waist, tempted to ask that she remove the sweater so he could get a good look at her nicely rounded curves.

This whole flirtatious thing he and Kamari had going was all Princess's fault. Four months ago, Princess had come home from a night partying with her *Real Baddies* castmates to find Markio and Kamari in the family room battling it out over a game of *Call of Duty: Modern Warfare*. Horny for some reason unknown to Markio, Prinny had kneeled between his black and white Amiri sneakers, opened his Amiri jeans and sucked him off right in front of her sister, slurping, jerking, and deepthroating him until his gooey semen exploded from her nostrils and sent her sprinting off to the nearest bathroom.

Kamari had gawked at his spastic erection in the moments thereafter, until his hard eleven inches became a soft six inches, and she'd been flirting with him ever since.

But this was the first time she ever sat on his lap.

"Prinny and I," Kamari said, exhaling a plume of smoke and reaching around under one arm to pass Markio the blunt, "we kinda have a fucked up history when it comes to boyfriends. She took my first real boyfriend from me when I was only thirteen. Fucked him in a gangway next to his older brother's house on Fifty Sixth and Michigan, and after that they dated for about two months. She claimed he was too old for me, because they were both fifteen, but she was really just a dick-hungry lil thot like all the rest of her friends. Then, two years ago, when I had this boyfriend named Jabar, we all flew down to Miami and spent the night drinking and smoking at this Airbnb, and she ended up locking herself in the bathroom with him for like twenty minutes. I could hear them through the door, and when she came out, she had cum on her chin."

"Damn, for real?" Markio puffed and passed, his brow raised in genuine surprise.

"Mm-hm. Nasty, ain't she?"

Markio only shook his head. His dick was like a snake frozen solid. He slid one hand around her narrow waist and down between her thick, dark thighs, stroking her pussy through the diaphanous fabric of her yoga shorts.

"I got a little payback with her last boyfriend," Kamari went on. "Sucked his dick the night before he went to jail for those two counts of attempted murder. I don't really feel like that was enough payback, though. What do you think?"

"Insufficient payback, that's what I thi—"

"WHAT IN THE *FUCK* ARE Y'ALL DOING?!"

The roaring voice belonged to Princess Joya Kelly, who'd just appeared in the open doorway of Markio's study with her hands on the hips of her stained white dress and her venomous gaze fixed on her backstabbing sister and her cheating boyfriend.

Chapter 8

Three o'clock.

Queen of Diamonds was dark and vacant.

All of the dancers and bartenders were gone, and the last of the janitors had left the building ten minutes ago.

The only lights that were still on inside the sprawling redbrick building were the ceiling fixtures of Weezy's second-floor office and the tubular fluorescent bulbs that spanned the length of the blue carpeted hallway leading up to his office door.

Weezy sat behind his desk with his face twisted in a malevolent sneer, scribbling his signature on the stack of papers Big Gabby had just handed him without really looking at them. Not that he really *needed* to look at them; he'd signed the same fuckin' papers a thousand times before. Checks and balances. Contracts for the newest dancers on QOD'S roster, and renewal for some of the more seasoned ones. A response to the Tyson food distributor that had nearly doubled the price on its cases of hot wings. Half a dozen legal notices that Weezy had absolutely no interest in reading over.

"I should be in to do the bank to drop at around noon," Big Gabby said. "Maybe twelve thirty. Blitz and that girl he's with finally moved back into their apartment so I should be able to get some sleep."

"You ever get hold of Fat Perry?" Weezy asked without looking up at her. "See what him and Aqua n'em got into?"

"I did but I didn't, if that makes any sense."

It didn't.

"He answered the phone, but he was mad as shit about some'n. Said somebody had side-swiped him and knocked the bumper off the front of his car. He was doin' way too much, so I hung up on his big, angry ass. I'll talk to him when he come in."

Weezy's unfriendly sneer morphed into a nefarious glare that seemed to emanate from the deep crease between his eyebrows. His lower lip, wet and shiny, eased out in front of the upper one. He tried vehemently to sign his name beside every 'X' Big Gabby had drawn on the papers, and he was getting through them at an agreeable enough pace, but the thing was, his signature no longer looked like *his* signature. Losing his right hand and then having it reattached had shot the nerve endings to perdition. His previously neat and legible handwriting had given way to chicken scratch.

By the time he made it through all the papers and looked up at Big Gabby, he was visibly enraged.

Big Gabby didn't notice, because like most people these days, her face was buried in her phone.

"The local alderman for the district brought up QOD's track record with the Chicago Police Department in some meeting he had with Mayor Johnson—you know, the few robberies we've had in the parking lot. And the few car thefts we had before we tripled up on razor wire," Gabby said from her seat on the opposite side of Weezy's large oak desk. "Anyway, Mayor Johnson had a little talk with the police superintendent, and now we have a police detail keeping an eye on our business. Sergeant Martin, the slim guy from somewhere in Rwanda, is in charge of the detail. I haven't met all the officers, but this one Haitian lady named Officer Pierre seemed pretty cool. She comes in from time to time, talks with the girls. She's good people." A pause as she swiped down her Instagram newsfeed. Then: "Daaamn. Did you get a look at all the people who showed up at Alexus Costilla's party? Jesus Christ."

"Jesus was there?" Weezy asked, his tone dripping with sarcasm, his pudgy face still a twisted mask of rage.

Big Gabby snorted a laugh. "I wouldn't be surprised if he *was*. I'll tell you that she had Young Nya up in that piece. Queen Bey, Angel Reese. Nicki. I don't see Millionaire Markio in none of the videos, but Princess got her lucky ass into the party. Looks like she was the only one from The Real Baddies who made it onto the guest list. Lucky ho."

Weezy picked up the gold-barreled ink pen he'd just finished scribbling with and launched it at Big Gabby's face, but sadly, like his handwriting, his aim wasn't what it used to be. The pen went high and wide, soaring through the air like a majorette's baton, and landed two feet outside of his open office door, stabbed the hallway carpeting like a miniature cenotaph.

It was only the squeak of his chair that alerted Big Gabby to the throw. She looked up just in time to watch the pen go cartwheeling over her head, the apogee reaching above the doorframe before arching back down and into the hallway.

"Nigga," she said, her voice pitched high with disbelief. She stood up, slipping her phone into her purse. "What was that about?"

"Get these papers and get out my office." Weezy growled.

"You seriously need to go and get your head checked out. For real though. We just had a good ass night, everybody's all happy to see you back, and yet you wanna come in here and throw a tantrum like a big ass toddler. For what? What's the goddam reason?"

"Millionaire Markio," he said mockingly. "That's all I hear from you raggedy bitches. Millionaire Markio did this. Millionaire Markio did that." Giving his best vocal imitation of an irritating women's voice. "Millionaire Markio wrote another book. He got a movie out." His regular voice returned with a vengeance. *"You ignorant bitches fail to mention how he had his uncle cut my motherfuckin' hand off!"*

Big Gabby let out an exasperated sigh. "Grow up, Weezy. Grow UP. That old-ass man— Herb or whatever the fuck– is Markio's uncle by marriage. Not blood. And besides, the old man thinks Markio was behind baby Stone's murder, and Baby Stone is Herb's nephew *by blood.* I heard that from Thick Doll. Baby Stone was her baby daddy."

She went out into the hallway and bent over to pick up Weezy's ink pen, and despite his outrage, he stared longingly at her enormous rump, thoroughly appreciating the view.

His fury, however, remained ruthlessly intact.

"Markio's a good man," Gabby said, rising back up with the pen in hand. "When I needed the money to pay for that lifesaving cancer removal procedure, he gave it to me, no questions asked. Saved my *life.* So yeah, I have a soft spot for him, and since Princess is his girl now, I guess I've developed a bit of a soft spot for her, too."

Weezy didn't much care for Big Gabby's so-called soft spots, as she soon found out. She placed his pen in the little black cup that held his other pens and markers and then, smiling amicably, she reached across his desk to get the papers he'd signed. His left arm shot out like a King Cobra, lunging out to sink its venomous fangs into the flesh of an unsuspecting prey. His left hand—his *good* hand–caught Big Gabby's wrist and squeezed with fingers that were strong enough to bend steel, yanking back so violently that she came sliding across his desk. His computer monitor survived the slide, but everything else— his cup of writing utensils, his keyboard and mouse, his desktop calendar, his half empty bottle of Hennessy and the stack of papers he'd signed with the erratic penmanship of a man suffering from Parkison's disease—went crashing to the floor. Big Gabby screamed, landing upside down in the debris, but Weezy kept twisting her wrist, applying pressure.

"You got a soft spot for that nigga? Hmm?"

Her answer came in the form of a scissor kick that slammed the toe of her high heeled shoe into the hollow of Weezy's temple. The blow, as unexpected as it was painful, stunned him. He released his iron grip on her wrist and growled like a pirate, instinctively bringing his injured hand up to press against the ache in his temple, wincing and clenching his teeth as the pain reverberated through his skull. He moved to stand. He only managed a slight forward hunch, his ass barely two inches off the seat of his chair, before he was promptly greeted with a vicious knee to the groin that doubled him over to the floor like a Muslim in prayer.

He let out another piratical growl.

"Thought I was just goin' to let you beat up on me again? Big Gabby straightened her dress and started collecting the signed papers from the floor. "How'd you like that scissor kick? Learned that one from my personal trainer. He teaches self-defense classes, too. Name's John Byers. You should give him a call."

"Bitch, I'ma... Bitch… I'ma …" *Kill you* was how Weezy wanted to finish that sentence, he just couldn't get it out with his testicles lodged behind his Adam's apple, or so it seemed.

"You. Ain't. Gon'. Do. Shit." Gabby said with all the ratchet gesticulations of a veteran hood rat. "Put your hands on me again and see if I don't put a forty caliber round right up your motherfuckin' ass."

And out the door she went. This Weezy knew because he fell over onto his side two seconds later, cradling his throbby gonads in the palm of his zombie right hand and thus was able to watch through the cubbyhole under his desk as she stormed off down the hallway, only instead of just one Big Gabby, he was seeing three— two clearly defined Gabby's flanking, the more blurry-looking one in the middle. He blinked hard and when he opened his eyes the three Gabby's merged into one. He shut his eyes and kept them that way until the throbbing waves of pain in his groin receded to a more tolerable level and then staggered to his feet, scooping up his half-gallon bottle of Cognac and steadying himself against his heavy oak desk.

"God *damn*," he said, the utter disbelief in his tone wringing a small grin from his scowl. "That fat bitch kicked the *shit* outta me. She kicked the *shit* outta me."

There were five blue doors on each side of the hallway leading up to Weezy's office. They were the Blue Rooms—the suavely furnished rooms where strippers brought their customers for private dances. Blue Room #6, which was just outside Weezy's office door on the left, was rarely used for private dancers, because it was the room where two or three of Weezy's fellow gang members usually sat in wait, in case the big man ever needed a helping hand.

Tonight there were two of them.

"You good in here, G?" Mondo asked as he and Wavy stepped into the office doorway.

They were dressed like the gangsters they were, in leather designer jackets over fitted jeans and designer sneakers. Cash shaped bulges protruded from their front pockets. Dreadlocks framed their battle-hardened young faces. Mondo was lanky and long faced, his skin the color of roasted peanuts. He was near thirty with the calculating maturity of someone twice his age. Wavy was darker, shorter, sillier. He had a gut on him, like Weezy, and was just three years out of high school. The melancholy of gang warfare had not yet begun to weigh on his features. He was applying the last few licks to the blunt he was rolling and judging from the pall of smoke that trailed them out of Blue Room #6, he and Mondo had already smoked quite a few of them.

"Did it *sound* like I was good in here?" Weezy snapped. "Big Gabby just pulled some Jet Li, Bruce Lee shit on me, nigga. Kicked me harder than a *mutha*fucka! I had that bitch right here." He pointed with the computer keyboard he'd just picked up. "Had her upside down, on her *neck*, and that bitch flipped right over and kicked my goddamn brains out. Then she kicked my balls way up in my chest somewhere. Long story short, *hell naw* I ain't good!"

Wavy snickered uncontrollably.

"Folks," said Mondo, "you told me not to get in between whatever you and your girl got going on. I'm only following orders."

"Orders? *Fuck some orders*! That ho just gave me a concussion. A-A-A fuckin' *brain* aneurysm, and you in here talking 'bout some goddam orders."

No more words were exchanged between Weezy and his cohorts. Mondo helped him pick up the debris. He killed the light, locked his office door, and took the stairs to the first floor, massaging the burgeoning knot on the side of his head as he passed Big Gabby's vacant office and threw open the rear exit door.

The Batur was the only vehicle still occupying a parking slot, but there were four sport utility vehicles idling close behind it. Two of them were dark colored Range Rovers. The other two were Jeep Grand Cherokee Trailhawks—or "Trackhawks" as they were more commonly known— and they were both matte black, with black wheels and even black windows.

Wavy and Mondo waited for Weezy to start up his Bentley coupe before they climbed into the rear seats of one Trackhawk, the one that was blaring drill music at three something in the morning.

For two or three minutes, forty-one-year-old Roy "Weezy" Sullivan sat quietly behind the wheel of his most recently acquired foreign toy, reveling in the glorious rumble of its 6.0 liter W-12 engine, raking his beady eyes over the drive mode dial and air vent organ stops that were made from hallmarked 18 karat gold. In those few minutes his anger at Big Gabby dwindled, like a bonfire with only a single charred branch smoldering in its ashes. She'd done nothing to deserve such harsh treatment. Millionaire Markio was equally undeserving of Weezy's wrath; he couldn't be blamed for his aunt's marital choices, and if it was true that he'd had a hand in Baby Stone's murder then the old man probably hated him, too.

The man responsible for Weezy' deformity was the 81-year-old Herbert Harris and soon Weezy vowed *very* soon he would track that old nigga down and sever one of his limbs, only it wouldn't be a measly hand.

Weezy typed out a heartfelt apology text to Big Gabby and sent it. Then he used the office security app on his phone to activate the club's alarm system, took a generous nip from his large bottle of Cognac, and went racing out of the parking lot with his gang in tow, slicing down Cottage Grove Avenue in a sleek violet sports car that no motorist or pedestrian he passed could even come close to affording.

And as he drove, he prayed.

"God, You know I ain't never asked for much. I can't even remember the last time I sent a prayer up there, but I need You today, so here it is: Please, God, *pleeease,* let me come face to face with the man who cut my hand off. That's all I ask. I'll take care of the rest myself."

It was 3:41A.M.

Chapter 9

Herbert Harris opened his eyes at 3:42 AM

A digital clock on his nightstand told him the time in glowing green numerals. In three minutes his alarm would sound, officially waking him for the day.

He closed his eyes and waited.

This is going to be a damned good Friday, Herb thought, and the lean, unsmiling man almost smiled.

His girls were gone. He'd heard their excited whispers even before they'd awakened him with the good news. The Haitian lady cop had messaged them saying Weezy had finally returned to lord over his high-class whorehouse, and Jaresha Brady had sent a dozen or more photos of the weasel's shiny new Bentley coupe.

And the good news didn't end there.

Karionna, the often loving and sometimes ill-tempered mother to her only living relative had messaged Herb saying that she had successfully planted a GPS tracker inside a load of cash she believed was en route to one of Millionaire Markio's stash houses. She'd also sent the description of both transport vehicles.

There was an old saying: *All bad things come in threes*.

Today, though, Herb thought the opposite might ring true, as well. He'd been in pursuit of Millionaire Markio for close to a year now, ever since the frigid December morning when Markio and four of his cronies caught him leaving his wife's primary place of residence, a single-family home made of redbrick and mortar in the quaint Chicago suburb of Hillside, Illinois. Herb had wanted him dead even before that— the whole thing had started when word got out that Markio put a bounty on the head of Jesse James Harris, Jr. AKA Baby Stone, over an unpaid drug debt—but it hadn't turned personal until Markio put a gun to Herb's jaw on the front porch of a home that should've been off limits.

He still remembered the threat.

Stay the fuck otta my b'ness, old school. This is only warning you gon' get. Baby Stone wanna be a gangsta. As soon as my shooters catch him outside, they gon' show him what it means to be a gangsta. And if I hear one more word about you tryna extort Weezy with that video, your old ass is gon' end up just like your nephew. We clear on that?

Less than two hours later, Herb had received a text from Harmonique Evans, the strikingly attractive Hyde Park native whose unyielding love and devotion to Baby Stone had earned her an engagement ring for the high-ranking mobster. The text message was short and to the point, just five words long, and yet it had taken all the air out of Herb's nicotine-stained lungs.

They just killed Baby Stone!

The five heartbreaking words were hanging there in front of his mind's eye when the alarm began its incessant series of beeps at exactly 3:45 A.M.

He swung his legs out of bed and sat up, reaching out to silence the alarm clock. He stretched and yawned and released a pungent fart that was heavily redolent of the three-bean chili he'd ingested the prior evening.

"Oh *man*," he said, fanning the air in front of his face. Maybe *pungent* was too mild of a word. His farts were like fire-breathing dragons. They were the main reason behind the girls' decision to flee his sleeping quarters for the vacant bedroom further down the hall.

The girls, Herb thought wistfully.

83

Tiffany Pires and Tylisha Coper, or TNT, as they were called by the folks on social media. Both twenty-seven, the girls shared the same dark complexion and slender physiques, and they'd been best friends since grammar school. Under Herb's tutelage, the two young women had become the successful owners of a combined fourteen rental properties with impressive stock portfolios to boot. They had gone from ghetto vagabonds to upper-class entrepreneurs and during their frequent visits to Herb's rural retreat— seventy densely wooded acres of land that had come with a 7,800 square feet log cabin in central Illinois— they had, to some degree, turned into the sort of women one could only find in the household of a military veteran. Herb had taught them all the things he had learned in Vietnam. Both women were equally proficient at cleaning, assembling, loading and discharging any firearm set before them. He'd even trained them in the use of high explosives, though their only real experience in that field had been the occasional exploding tree.

Today that would change.

Today, if Herb's plans came to fruition, the girls would more than earn the right to that explosive nickname of theirs.

Herb stood and stretched again. His various joints popped like firecrackers. Like most men in their early eighties, his limbs were prone to aches and pains that sometimes required a moufful of Ibuprofen to get the day going, especially on cold pre-winter mornings like today, when the outside temperature seemed to come right through the windowpanes and latch onto his every bone.

But this morning was notably different. Herb shuffled to the bathroom across the hall — a frail man of Micheal Blackson's complexion clad in baggy black boxers and slippers — with nary a groan, and when he returned to his bedroom twelve minutes later to make his bed the way he'd learned in the military—forty five degree angles at the foot end, five inches counterpane foldback at the head— he was feeling more fresh than he had in a very long time. He dressed himself in a dark green Brioni business suit with an emerald-colored silk tie, oxford shoes and a dark green thousand-dollar top hat with a pristine brown feather wedge in the left side. The feather matched his shoes, the smoothly polished wood of his walking cane, and the mildly scuffed leather of his shoulder holster, which held his large Beretta pistol, a Px4. 45. He clasped a shiny gold Audemars Piguet watch around his left wrist, slipped on his gold wedding ring, and strolled out into the green and blue tiled hallway with aplomb, his cane clicking rhythmically on the floor as he went.

It was a modest-sized condominium situated on the thirty-ninth floor of a nondescript high rise in the affluent Streeterville neighborhood near downtown Chicago. Herb was only leasing the condo. It set him back $4,500 a month, but the view was worth every dollar spent.

From his floor to ceiling kitchen window, he could see right across the street to Sheraton Suites, the glorious steel and glass skyscraper where, on the thirty-ninth floor, Roy "Weezy" Sullivan owned a swanky four bedroom condo fit for a king.

"It's gonna be a pretty shitty day for you, Weasel," Herb said, his raspy voice brimming with glee as he entered his kitchen and flicked a brief glance out that dark window. "A pretty shitty day, indeed."

The timer on his coffee machine was set for 3:55 A.M. A steaming mug of French roast awaited him. Tylisha was an excellent cook, and this morning she had left a plate of breakfast in the microwave. Poached eggs, grits, bacon and rye toast. Herb's iPhone lay charging on the granite paved countertop. He took his plate, his coffee, and his phone to the head of the round cherrywood table and sat with his chair at an angle, facing the wall of windows that were mirrored on the outside so that he could see out but no one out there could see in.

The Sheraton didn't have mirrored windows. The ones in Weezy's apartment had royal blue drapes hanging down to the floor like a long, ruffled dress. A pair of high tech binoculars— the kind that were capable of capturing video and photos of whatever he zoomed in on— lay next to the standing roll of paper towels in the center of Herb's kitchen table, and though he usually took some time out of each morning, afternoon, evening and night to pick up the binoculars and watch for any signs of movement inside Weezy's place, he didn't even consider doing it now.

He took his time eating a single slice of toast and two strips of bacon. Then he ripped loose a square of paper towel, wiped the oil form his lips and fingertips, picked up his cell phone, and read a text message from Tiffany that made him smile— an expression he wore so rarely that it felt foreign on his coal black face.

He made a FaceTime call to Weezy, and his smile widened a bit more when Weezy's round face appeared on his phone screen.

"Welcome home, Weasel! I was beginning to think you'd ran out on me. I've been lonely without you. How the hell are you?"

"You dead, old man." Weezy spoke with the unwavering conviction of a cold-blooded killer who has just come face to face with the scum who'd murdered his brother. He was driving, but he kept looking at Herb every couple of seconds. "I just said a prayer not even twenty five minutes ago, *beggin'* God to let me get up close and personal with yo' old ass. This ain't what I had in mind, but it's a start."

"I'd rescind that prayer if I were you."

"Nahh. I already sent it up, and God came through on His end. Now where you—"

"No, no, no. You dumb fuck. I said *rescind*. R-E-S-C-I-N-D, not resend as in send it again. Were your parents siblings? Hm? Brother and sister? Had to be for you to come out that big and stupid."

"You dead, old man," Weezy repeated, his face taut with rage. "On Larry Bernard Hoover, on the Gangster Disciple Nation and all my dead homies, as *soon* as we find out where yo' old ass been hiding, we gon' be at your front door."

At your front door came out at *cho front doe*.

Herb cackled at Weezy's rising anger. He thought of one of those old glass thermometers, the red vertical line soaring up, up, up until it smashed through the tip, maybe even through the roof of that sweet new coupe The Weasel was pushing. There was a deformity on the right side of Weezy's head, Herb noticed: a knot the size and shape of a crab apple.

"Aw, man," Herb said, biting into a second crunchy strip of bacon, "word on the street is that you put a hundred grand on my head. If I were you, I'd split that in half and put the other fifty grand on whoever broke their foot off in your ass."

The joke might have brought down the house at the Laugh Factory, but it did nothing for Weezy. His face remained as hard and stolid as a Stone Age cave dweller.

"You cut my fuckin' hand off."

"True." Herb pointed an accusatory finger at the camera. "But that was *after* the fact. *After* you reached for my throat." He saw the grease glistening on his finger and hastily swiped it across his used paper towel before raising it to point again. "You attacked, I counter-attacked, because that's the way war works. I may have crossed the line when I tried blackmailing you with that murder video; swearing I'd send it to the cops if you didn't take out Millionaire Markio, but that was only a threat. I was in a hard spot, so to speak. I had just learned that Markio was offering a shit load of money for somebody to murder my nephew, Baby Stone, and when I got hold of that video of you shooting Oats, I looked at it as an easy way out of a difficult situation. Of course, that didn't work out as planned. Baby Stone still wound up getting killed and Markio, who I'm sure had everything to do with it, is alive and well. But you see where I'm coming from?"

Weezy only sneered. He had either braked at a red light, pulled over to the side of the road, or arrived at his destination, because he was no longer driving. He stared at the octogenarian on the other end of the video call, not blinking, not even seeming to breathe.

"Now, now," Herb said, unable to suppress his overwhelming amusement. "Settle down. No need to get all bent outta shape. After all, it was your choice to drive out there to Roseland and kill that man in broad daylight, with nothing to cover your face when you did it. That, my friend, was an idiotic move— one of epic proportions I might add. You're the breadwinner, *Weasel*! You gotta be able to *think*."

"I'ma kill you," Weezy said, very matter-of-fact.

"Can you say anything else, or is your brainpower really that limited?" Herb shook his head, genuinely flummoxed by Weezy's poor communication skills. "Have you ever watched *Sanford and Son*? From now on, you can just call me Pop, and I'll call you Lamont, because you are one… big… dummy."

"Just tell me where to find you so we can go on and get this over with. I ain't wit' all this talkin." Weezy turned up a huge bottle of Hennessy and gulped down an ounce or so. Such a swallow would have scrunched Herb's face into a roadmap of wrinkles, but Weezy didn't so much as blink.

Herb stood and slapped his open hand down on the table, a sharp pistol clap sound that made Weezy flinch. No more Herb the Comedian. No more Mr. Nice Guy.

"Times up, Weasel!" Herb's eyes were savage, fuming. "You really want to play this game with *me*? Fine! Game on, dick sucker! Get all your affairs in order, get in as many hugs and kisses as you can fit into the next few hours, because as soon as I'm done taking a big shark bite out of Markio's little operation, I'm coming to *devour* you, and believe you me, there won't be an inch of you left for your loved ones to bury!"

"Is that s'pose to scare me, grandpa?"

"It *should* scare you. And do you know why?" Herb brought the phone closer to his furious old face. "You should be very fucking scared, Weasel, because remember I'm Pop, and you're Lamont, and this is The Big One!"

Chapter 10

"What if they have kids in there? What if there's some old lady sitting in her favorite arm chair, knitting ugly Christmas sweaters for her grandkids?"

Tiffany Pires, called "T" by most who know her, shrugged her narrow shoulders in a gesture of dismissal and drew her lips aside in contemplation. She was sitting in the driver's seat of a plain white commercial van. No windows in back, just the double doors. Tylisha sat in the passenger's seat, appearing less comfortable in her black polo AT& T shirt and slacks than Tiffany did in hers, staring straight ahead and across the street at the single story house with two black Escalades parked at the curb in front.

"I highly doubt this guy is going to have a bunch of kids or his grandma sitting around in the house where he hides all his drug money. That wouldn't make much sense," Tiffany reasoned.

"You never know." Tylisha countered, the trepidation in her tone as thick as a Mississippi swamp possum with the mumps. She sighed once, sighed twice. Wriggled her butt on the seat while exhaling a third sigh. "I don't know about that one, T. I really don't."

"It'll be fine."

Tiffany looked to her Apple smartwatch for the time. 4:09 A.M. She had parked the van near the corner of 15th Street and Trumbull Avenue, in the blighted Lawndale neighborhood on Chicago's west side. There was no more snowfall, but plenty of the stuff layered the barren lawns and broken patches of sidewalk. The sky was still a star-spangled blanket of darkness above, offering perfect cover to any ill-intentioned human beings below.

The package— a small brown cardboard box containing a half kilo of C4 explosive – lay on the front porch of the targeted house their Apple Air Tag GPS tracker had led them to. Tiffany had placed it there, wearing the black latex gloves and dark gray balaclava that she still had on. When detonated, Tiffany knew the C4 would travel outward at nineteen thousand miles per hour, almost sixty times the speed of sound: the vapors and blast wave would raze the building and reduce everything in its path to nothingness.

"This is like something out of an Ashley and JaQuavis novel," Tylisha said, slinking down in her seat. "You ever read *The Cartel*?" Tiffany nodded, and Tylisha added, "Herb got us out here like we're the Murder Mamis or some'n."

Tiffany said nothing. Her eyes were on the house, studying the dark windows, wondering if whomever resided there would awaken before the bomb was detonated.

"I'll tell you what," Tylisha said, rather crossly. "Blowing up trees is way, way, way different than blowing up an actual house with people in it. That's murder, T. Terrorism. And I ain't no motherfuckin' terrorist."

Again Tiffany said nothing. She turned on the radio, tuned to 92.3 FM, got Sexyy Red, and began to hum along. She considered firing up a cigarette and then remembered that both she and Tylisha had left their purses at home. Herb wouldn't have approved of her smoking at a time like this anyway. Cigarette butts held DNA.

Two minutes later Sexxy Red segued into Meek Mill. The beat was mediocre. But Meek did what he could with what he had. Tiffany adored the handsome young Philadelphia rap artist; she found herself smiling unconsciously at the aggressive sound of his voice. She had sided with him in the whole Meek Mill versus Drake beef, and over the years she'd squandered many of her hard-earned dollars on tickets to his shows, dishing out extra hundreds for front-row action.

Tylisha, who had thought to bring along a book— a dog-eared paperback entitled *A Thugs Street Princess 2*, by Meesha— now opened it to read.

"Meek Mill wrote a book, too," Tiffany said. "*Tony Story*. I read it twice. Think it's still on the bookshelf at my sister's house."

"I saw the movie. Watched it with Crunchy before he got killed. I like it."

An uncomfortable silence ensured. Crunchy was an ex-boyfriend of Tylisha's who lost his life in a hail of gunfire in his very own neighborhood after leaving a nearby gas station in a stolen car. There was an ongoing rumor that Nya Mixon, the famous MBM rap artist who now went by Young Ny, was responsible for Crunch's murder— several eyewitnesses had reported seeing a young woman matching Nya's description hop out of a Jeep and fire a Draco pistol into the driver's window of Crunch's stolen car—but no arrests had ever been made.

The silence was broken three minutes later when the burner phone on Tiffany's lap twittered. It was Herb. "That thing in place?"

"You know it," Tiffany said, delighted.

"Good." There was a modicum of anger in his raspy old voice. "Get a good distance away, at least a block or two. Then you dial that number and give 'em hell."

"That's a big ten-four." Tiffany replied. Like some redneck trucker.

She ended the call, started the engine, and drove forward, obeying the stop sign before crossing 15th Street and continuing onto the next street, which was Douglas Boulevard. Her warm brown eyes began to feed off Tylisha's apprehension, glittering with joy as she rounded the corner and stepped down on the brake, stopping the van so that, through Tylisha's window, they would both have an unobstructed view of the stash house from a block and a half away.

Tiffany pulled up the phone number.

Tylisha gasped, her eyes as wide and round as silver dollars.

"Boom goes the dynamite," Tiffany said, and hit CALL.

The explosion was immediate and deafening. And *huge*. At first all Tiffany could see where the red brick house had been was a great plume of fire blossoming out of the darkness, like a mini Hiroshima. Then the blast rocked the earth—rocked the whole *world*, it seemed— and sent one of the Escalades cartwheeling to the opposite side of the street, where it landed upside down on top of someone's dented-up Kia sedan, like a *Hot Wheels* toy truck some outraged toddler had kicked across the floor. The second Escalade and two other vehicles that had been parked near the blast site were blown sideways and tipped over onto their sides.

And then came the debris, clumps of brick and dirt and God knew what else, raining down like hailstones on everything within a two-block radius. Every car alarm on the street was activated.

A fat chunk of cinder block came crashing down onto the street just outside Tiffany's door, and she stamped down on the gas pedal.

Chapter 11

So you mad now? Bc u caught me SITTING on ur man's lap?! How many of my bfs have u fucked again? And yes that includes the 1 who throat fucked u in Miami and left his cum on ur face! MISS ME W/THAT BULLSHIT!!!

The text message had been delivered at 3:05 AM and read two minutes later. Maybe ten minutes after Princess had lifted her sleeping daughter out of bed and left right back out of Markio's mansion, stopping to order his guy Bam to give her a ride in his blacked-out Rolls-Royce Cullinan. Kamari knew this only because she and Markio had stood there behind his desk and watched the camera, Kamari with her hands on her hips and her mouth hanging open, Markio wearing an amiable grin and taking deep pulls from his blunt. It was the same expression he'd worn when Kamari jumped off his lap at the sound of Prinny's enraged shout.

Just over an hour had passed since Kamari had sent that text, an hour of crying and crying for no fucking reason, lying in bed with her knees drawn up to her chest and her daddy's old sweater pulled down over them. Feeling horrible for betraying the half-sister who'd done the very same thing to her on *numerous* occasions. It was like Judas Iscariot calling Jesus Christ a traitor instead of the other way around. Pure fucking hypocrisy.

Sniffling, Kamari wiped the tears from her eyes with the damp sleeve of her sweater. She got on her phone and checked all of Prinny's social media pages– TikTok,

Facebook, Instagram, Thread, X and Snapchat— to see if the bitch had posted anything since she'd taken off with the so-called "Chief" of the faction of TVL Markio ran with. There were no disparaging posts. No posts at all in fact.

"Damn right," Kamari murmured, nodding her head on her silk encased pillow. "I wish you would get online and try to throw some shade at me. I'll expose that ass like some crotchless leggings. Play with me if you want to."

A knock at her door. She rolled over and looked at it, considering. Here she was lying in a king-size canopy bed with red frilled curtains flowing down from the cherrywood bedposts like menses redolent of fabric softener in a richly furnished bedroom with its own private bathroom and walk-in closet that was larger than the two-bedroom apartment she'd grown up in with Princess and their mother, and she was only considering a voiced answer to the man on the opposite side of the door, the man who was allowing her to live rent-free in his Lincoln Park mansion.

Maybe she was a horrible person.

"You woke in there?" Markio asked, then, "I don't know why I even said that when I just heard you talking through the door. This oak might be thick as you, but it ain't soundproof."

That got a low-spirited laugh out of Kamari. "Come in, boy." She said sitting up and back against three large pillows.

Markio pushed open the door and stood there in the doorway, the way Princess had paused, frozen at the threshold of the office door. He'd added a T-shirt and the matching Louis Vuitton hoodie to his outfit and switched out the flip flops for an all-white pair of Air Max '95 sneakers, but other than that he looked the same, his double cup of Lean in the one hand, another blunt of the good stuff in the other. The refractive display of VVS diamonds he wore around his neck, wrists and pinkie finger created an awe-inspiring array of colors.

Kamari could see all this only because of the light spilling in from the hallway behind him. She had turned off the lights in her bedroom, intent on crying herself to sleep.

"I ain't no muhfuckin' boy," Markio said, and sipped. "I'm a grown-ass man, dog. A grown-ass man." Like Cedric the Entertainer.

Kamari rolled her yes, sucked a tooth and sighed all at the same time, a black women's sign of irritation if ever there was one. "What do you want, shortstop?"

"I lost some'n on the roof. Need you to reach up there and get it."

Kamari laughed in the dark. "You are so stupid." She sniffed, wiping her eyes. "I've been in here crying my eyes out this whole time."

"Prinny ain't called?"

"Nope, and I don't know where she's at. I checked the cameras at our place in Highland Park, and she's not there. Not that she'd go there anyway, with all the renovations going on. Wouldn't be safe for Vee."

"I know where she went." Markio said stepping into the bedroom. "We shared locations up until about fifteen minutes ago. She was at Aqua's house out there in Burr Ridge when it cut off. Told Bam not to tell me where he dropped her off. But I had already seen it."

Kamari gave another suck of her teeth. This time it was more perfunctory than from any specific emotion. She was still high as a kite. Her eyes were bloodshot and squinted, and her tongue felt like sandpaper. She had a family size bag of sour Skittles in her nightstand drawer. She dug it out, dumped some in her hand, and popped a few in her mouth as Markio leaned back against her bureau, lighting his blunt and staring down at the flame as he did it, lost in his own rueful thoughts.

"I didn't check that notification," he said, slowly and dolefully bringing the blunt to his mouth for a long, hard pull. When he spoke again his voice was scratchy from all the smoke he was holding in. "The camera at the first front gate. They automatically take pictures of every person or vehicle coming in or leaving. Sends 'em right to my phone. It was just that... Well, you know... You had all that ass on me. Shit threw me off my square. Made me lose focus for a minute." Smoke poured out of his nose.

"I'm so sorry, Markio," Kamari said, and she really was... although it did feel kind of good to know that her body possessed such power.

"Nah, that was all on me. I'm a grown man. Shit, I'll be forty in a couple years. I'm old enough and mature enough to take responsibility for my own actions. I let you sit on my lap because that's where I wanted you to sit. I mean, who wouldn't want you on their lap? I didn't want you to get up!"

He chuckled once and then crossed the floor to the corpulent Italian leather davenport that stood before the foot-end of Kamari's bed, spanning the entire width of it. He sat down. Sipped and puffed. Tipped his head back and blew a line of smoke toward the ceiling.

Smiling more radiantly now, Kamari slipped out of bed, her bare feet sinking into the warm red carpet. She took the pink and red Hello Kitty ashtray from her nightstand and brought it to Markio, cradling her iPhone and bag of Skittles against her chest.

"Well, if it makes you feel any better," she said plopping down next to him, "I didn't really wanna get up either. She startled me, that's why I jumped up."

She placed the ashtray on his thigh and reached for the blunt, pulling her legs up beneath her. This time he surrendered it without hesitation. She had only taken one toke when it occurred to her that her bedroom door was ajar. She got up, closed the door, locked it and returned to her seat.

"Bitch won't be poppin' up in my doorway." She said, staring at the profile of Markio's handsome face and waiting for her eyes to adjust to the gloom. He was wearing that grin of his, shaking his head, slouched back on the sofa with his eye on the high ceiling.

"She shouldn't have sucked my dick in front of you," he said. After a time, "That's really what started this hit between us."

"Exactly!" Kamari exclaimed, dumping the blame on Prinny. "I was sitting there, you know, all the way in my zone, kickin' your ass at *Call of Duty*—"

"That's a goddamn lie."

"When all of a sudden this drunk bitch comes in and drops to her knees between your legs. I couldn't fuckin believe it. She opened your pants and dragged out the biggest dick on the planet, sucked it until cum-snot blasted out of her nose and then she expects me not to want a sample." She passed him the blunt, staring down at his crotch in search of a phallic print.

"We ain't gon' just skip over that part about you supposedly kickin' my ass at *Call of Duty*. You *know t*hat didn't happen."

Kamari seemed not to hear. "That dick felt so long and fat under my ass. Boy, you had my pussy so wet. My nipples were so hard." She licked her lips. "Mm-mm-mm. Let me quit before I start somethin'."

Her titillating words achieved the desired effect: the flaccid length of meat in Markio's pants began to rise and fill out, like a slowly inflating balloon. The kind circus clowns tied into animals.

"Gucci Ball and Cocky Lord was just talkin' about you before they pulled off," Markio said turning to gaze at her. "They say you look like that WNBA player who on *NBA Today* all the time."

Kamari smiled at the comparison. "Chiney something. She got an African last name. So many people tell me I look like her. I can see the resemblance. Somewhat. We're both tall and dark-skinned, with fat around asses and pretty faces. My face is more rounded, though, and I think I might be a shade darker." She paused, staring wantonly at the conspicuous outline of his growing erection, then blurted, "I might can't suck dick like Prinny, but I got good pussy. Good pussy."

"Ah yeah?"

"Yup, Wet-wet and I bet you this, too: you can't hit it from the back and last I know that for a fact."

"You don't know shit. The fuck I look like, a minute man to you or some'n?" He smashed his blunt out in the ashtray and stood up, sipping from the cup in his left hand, thumbing down the front of his sweatpants and underwear with his right hand.

His cock sprang out, thick and hard and inconceivably long. It bobbed around for a moment, like one of those springy old doorstops. Kamari's mouth fell agape in a gasp that Markio immediately took advantage of, taking the back of her head in his free hand and thrusting his dick in over her retracted tongue and way to the back of her throat.

"Yeahhh," he said, like Young Jeezy on a track. "Let me see what that throat feel like."

Kamari gagged, her eyes went wide, and her eyebrows, masterfully groomed by the stellar cosmetologist at Mamah's Salon on a bi-weekly basis for two hundred dollars per session, rose to her forehead as Markio's huge black cock settled into her throat, effectively sealing off her airway. She threw her phone and her bag of chewy confections aside and began smacking her open hands on his hips; in her panic she forgot all about the few individual Skittles she'd had in her other hand and they went tumbling down Markio's right pantleg.

Finally, just as the candy she'd ingested and the jerk chicken meal she'd eaten for dinner began their ascent up her esophagus like a couple of novice rock climbers negotiating a steep incline, Kamari managed to shove Markio with enough force to dislodge his dick from the previously unexplored depths of her virgin throat.

"Fucker!" She glared up at him, panting and swallowed down the mass of bile that had started to rise. "*Don't* do that!"

"Damn, a'ight. My bad," he said, raising his free hand in surrender and rocking that dumb shit smirk he worked so well. "I get it. Hands off approach. You can go ahead and do you."

Kamari's cold stare faded away and her radiant smile resurfaced, because the ho in her rather liked the idea of choking on a fat black dick. She returned her eyes to the prize, and oh what a glorious prize it was. She gathered up some spit, which was quite easy, with her mouth watering the way it was and oozed it out along the top part of his considerable length. She gave it a few good, twisting strokes, working two or three more inches into her mouth and began rocking her head forward and back. Giving it a lot of suction, and a lot of tongue and a lot of spit. Keeping one hand on his waist to keep him from thrusting forward, the other hand stroking and twisting as she sucked him.

"Ah yeah," he said, nodding his head approvingly. "Ah yeeeeahh. That's it right there. On King Neal. On Cup Gang. That's it right there. Eat it up." A series of unintelligible mumblings later, he cleared up and added, "You fuckin' liar. Talking' about you don't know how to suck dick. Like my mama always say, you's a lie and the truth ain't in you."

She took her mouth off him, laughed faintly, and jokingly said, "Shut the fuck up… before I bite it off. And don't nut in my mouth."

Markio pushed out his lower lip in a pout but said nothing in protest. Perhaps her threat, though spoken in jest, had registered in his brain as something to be taken seriously. Whatever the case, Kamari squeezed his meat in her fist and continued fellating him, enjoying the rubbery feel of it gliding in and out of her mouth relishing the salty taste of pre cum on her tongue.

Only a short time had passed when Markio phone rang in his pocket. He dug it out, and Kamari was able to see the name Weezy on the screen before Markio raised the phone to his ear.

"Yooooo, Weezy Wee. What's up, joe?" There was a muted reply. "Shit, gettin' my dick sucked. Man, I told you before buddy ain't no kin to me. Just 'cause he married my auntie don't make him my uncle. He said he gon' do what?"

Markio listened intently, looking down at Kamari with his teeth biting down into the center of his bottom lip. She was only vaguely aware of his lingering gaze, because at that moment her own cell phone buzzed to life on the sofa cushion beside her. She turned to look at it, taking Markio's dick from the side like corn on a cob, and saw it was her boyfriend. Malcom Stephen, the rakishly handsome part-owner of Red Eye Surprise, a Wicker Park marijuana dispensary. A former pugilist, he'd once owned a World Boxing Association light heavyweight title belt and had an impressive record of seventeen consecutive knockouts.

He and Kamari had met on the BLK dating app, and after three months of dating, they'd decided to take their burgeoning friendship to a more intimate level. Which was when Kamari began to regret ever swiping right on Malcom "The Blur" Stephens to begin with. He may have been a championship contender in the ring but below the belt he was a real disappointment. His dick measured all of five inches when fully erect, he had yet to last more than five minutes in bed, and though he thoroughly enjoyed receiving oral sex, as the son of a white Presbyterian woman and an eccentric black Jamaican father who'd taught him zilch about the birds and bees, Malcolm simply "did not believe in" going down on a woman.

Kamari reached out to silence her phone and then began using it to record video of herself sucking Markio's dick. Something she could and would masturbate to later.

"Man, ain't nobody worried about that old-ass nigga. He just talkin, Weezy. Don't let that bullshit get under your skin," Markio was saying. "Yup.. Yup… and good looking on the warning about them Hobos. I'll worry about them before I worry about that old-ass man… Yup, one."

Markio was reaching to slip his phone back into his pocket when it rang again. This time, Kamari noted the name on his phone was Big J.

"Maan, they got me fucked up," he said and powered his phone off completely. "It's four some'n in the morning; and now niggas wanna start callin' me and shit."

"Who's Big J?"

"That's Jessica. This chick I grew up with on Trumbull. My older sister best friend." He shuddered and took two steps back, snatching dick from inside Kamari's tightly pumping first. "Damn," he said breathing shakily. "Wait a minute. Shit. You gon' make me nut."

Kamari rose from the sofa, wiping the slobber from around her mouth and peeling off her shorts. Let's get in this bed. See if I can jam my pussy to the back of *your* throat."

"Don't threaten me with a good time."

Leaving his stacked cups on her dresser, Markio shucked his outfit and climbed in bed wearing only his Versace boxers shorts, his socks and his blinging diamond jewelry. Kamari tossed her oversize sweater and the OTF "Free Smurk" tee she'd worn under it, rendering her completely naked.

"Turn on the lights," Markio said, kneeling on the bed.

"Alexa, turn on the lamps," Kamari said, lying back on her pillows with her thick legs folded back and two fingers caressing the damp petals of her labia. The lights flicked on and she gasped at the unthinkable length of the brick hard penis sticking out from between Markio's legs.

"Daaaamn. It looks even bigger in the light!"

Markio chuckled his amusement, biting down on his bottom lip again, staring long and hard at her jumbo breasts, tight waistline, and voluminous dark thighs.

"Goddamn," he marveled.

Kamari considered coaxing him forward, but there was no need. He did it on his own, moving forward on his knees with his bloodshot eyes on her smoothly shaved pussy as if it had somehow hypnotized him. He wet his lips, smiled up at her, and lowered his mouth for a taste. First, he kissed on the hood of her clitoris. Then, with his first two fingers he pushed back the hood and placed a soft slow tongue kiss on the pinkish little nub itself.

That was when, miraculously, Kamari's head fell backward, her mouth yawned wide, and she cried out in orgasm— the fastest orgasm she'd ever achieved.

She was unable to pinpoint the exact reason behind her premature climax. It could have been the gradual buildup of sexual arousal that had started in Markio's study, calmed down for about an hour, and then fired back up again as she sat sucking his dick a few moments ago; or maybe it was the sheer anticipation of knowing that it was only a matter of minutes before she would be skewered on his gigantic horse dick like a pig on a rotisserie— but no matter the underlying reason there was no denying the overall results. She most certainly had an orgasm as she screamed like a woman being murdered. She dug her fingernails into the tattoo on the side of Markio's left forearm, a scowling Chucky doll holding an AK-47, and when he kept licking on her clit, she punched him three times on the head, in rapid succession.

Whop Whop Whop

"Ahh! Bitch!" He scooted away before her fourth blow could land and rubbed the top of his head where she'd socked him, messing up his low-cut waves. "You just punched the shit outta me." His grin spread into a smile so wide that she could see all his teeth.

Kamari began to laugh, breathing fast and haltingly. "I'm so sorry. That never happened to me before. I swear."

"Well," he said, shuffling forward on his knees again, stroking his sizable appendage in one hand. "You just fucked that up. On bro. That shit is over with."

"I'm so sorry," Kamari repeated.

"It's all good. Don't even trip. Payback is a Maybach."

Markio was still smiling, showing two rows of perfect white chompers that were obviously veneers- very expensive veneers, no doubt- but he spoke in a threatening undertone, rubbing his fat cockhead up and down between her slippery vaginal lips. Her jaw hung low with anticipation, and as he began to push it in deeper, she sucked in a breath and held it.

What came next was like giving birth in reverse.

Maybe that was hyperbole, since Kamari had never actually given birth herself, but that was the best way she could describe the feeling of Markio entering her. She'd never been stretched so wide and deep. Not even during her pubescent years, when she'd taken anything even quasi-phallic in shape- cucumbers, television remotes, even a few broomsticks and the uniquely slanted handle of a vacuum— and jammed it up her coochie for relief. No, what Markio had going on below the belt was something otherworldly. A black human dick of superhuman proportions, and as he began rocking his hips back and forth, sliding his super dick in and out of her, real tears formed in her eyes, and she murmured breathlessly, "I love you already."

It was love at first fuck.

"Aw, you love me now, huh? You love me now. Just punched me all on top of my goddamn head a minute go, but now you love a nigga" The speed and depth of his thrust increased. His necklaces, swinging freely as he leaned in over her with her legs pinned back, made that metallic chinging sound, the icy incrustations of the attached pendants flickering through every color on the color wheel. MILLIONAIRE MARKIO, read one pendant; HOLY CITY, read another, which Kamari knew was a nickname for the North Lawndale neighborhood where he was born and raised. A third pendant read CUP GANG in lettering that was nearly identical to the tattoo he had arched across his belly. "Nah, you don't love me. You don't love me at all. You love this *dick* already. That's what you love. This dick."

And maybe he was right
A single, salty tear trickled down from her left eye and dripped into her ear.

She moaned in short, sporadic yips, like a dog being smacked around by its abusive owner. She hated the sound and wished she'd had the foresight to turn on some music. She still could. All it would take was another command to Alexa, her ever helpful computer assistant. But that would require a pause in the coochie stretching, skin clawing round of fucking she and Markio were engaged in, and there was no way in hell she was going to do that.

She creamed her way through a second orgasm ten or twelve minutes later. Markio called her all kinds of nasty bitches as she did it, and this time when she balled her fist, he took hold of her forearm and forced it against her chest.

"Nah, nahh, nigga," he said with a knowing smirk. "Won't be gittin' me again. Not today."

Kamari would have laughed if not for her screaming moans. Markio slipped out of her and sat back on his haunches, jacking his super dick and waiting on her to regain her composure. When she did, he ordered to her to turn over.

"We gon' see if I can't hit it from the back and last," he said, and Kamari knew right then that he could. Could and would. All the facts were there: Millionaire Markio really was a superhuman, if only in the bedroom.

Kamari was sapped of energy. Even so, she managed to summon up the strength to roll over and pull herself up on her knees, leaving the side of her head sunken into her pillow. She threw a command Alexa's way while Markio positioned himself behind her. GloRilla came on rapping about slapping rap bitches and making bail and the volume was up loud enough to eclipse Kamari's squealing moans as Markio slid in and took her to Pound Town.

Due to the blaring music, and also due to the vast distance between Kamari's bedroom, which overlooked the courtyard in the north wing of Markio's sprawling mansion, and the massive twenty car garage, which sat outside the west wing, neither he nor Kamari heard the gunshots.

Chapter 12

Jahlil Owens was the first one in the circle of dice rollers to receive news of the Trumbull Avenue explosion. His wife, Tirazh, had seen video of the burning eggshell of a building on her Facebook news feed and tagged him in the post.

"What the Fuuuuck," he said in a voice so low it might have been a whisper. The video filmed by Jessica Mensam, Jah presumed, since it was posted to her Facebook page, began as Jessica, holding her phone in one shaky hand, descended the rickety wooden staircase to her first floor living room and gasped at the sight of her blown in window and all the destructive chunks of rubble that littered her previously immaculate tan leather sofas and chairs, her coffee table and her tan colored carpet. Fragments of glass lay among shattered pieces of red brick, and her flat screen TV looked like someone had used it for practice at a gun range.

"Oh my God," Jessica narrated. Her voice was even shakier than her hand. "It's the same upstairs. All the windows, shattered. Sounded like a goddamn bomb went off! If my generator hadn't kicked in, I wouldn't even have no lights. Oh my God, I'm so glad my kids ain't here. Deadbeat baby daddy came through for me this time, I give him that."

She opened a door that led out to an enclosed porch and panned her camera across a similar path of destruction. Only there was something else scattered among all the glass and brick.

"Is that … Is this a fifty dollar bill?"

Jah figured it out before Jessica did. She moved her camera close to the floor and saw that it was indeed a fifty dollar bill- burned to a crisp around the edges and ripped nearly in half, but a fifty dollar bill, nonetheless.

And there were others. Two twenties and a hundred lay smoldering on the seat of a wicker chair, and the pink little bicycle leaning against the opposite wall had another charred fifty draped over the pink right-hand grip of its handlebars

"Joe, look at this shit," Jah said, jamming an elbow into the flabby gut of his fat friend Apple, who at the moment seemed to be engaged in a romantic slow dance with the extra-large bucket of KFC chicken to his chest. "Don't Jessica still live on Trumbull?"

"Maan. Watch them sharp-ass elbows, Lord. Fore I fuck around and chicken slap yo lil black ass," Apple threatened jokingly, for no man in his right mind would ever consider threatening Jah seriously. Sinking his strength into a crunchy skinned drumstick, Apple leaned in over Jah's phone to watch Jessica Mensa's video, just as Luke the Producer, whose parents still resided at 1524 South Trumbull Avenue, stood up from his kneeled position next the dice game to answer a call from his old man.

Kitty Jae stood just a few inches to Jah's left, her arms crossed and her eyes on his phone. Her boyfriend, Anton, was crouched low in a squat just ahead of her, shaking the dice between his knees as if he were beating off, trying earnestly to win back the two thousand dollars he'd lost since they first arrived twenty or thirty minutes ago.

He and Kitty had lucked their way into an invitation to Millionaire Markio's extravagant Lincoln Park mega-mansion. Kitty Jae had told Anton everything, and Anton had immediately phoned Markio's cousin, Sawbuck, who'd invited them to the house of Lords to deliver the news in person.

"He should be back down here in a minute," Sawback had told them when they first walked into the garage. "He just went back in the crib a few minutes ago. Going through some bullshit with is girl right now."

Kitty Jae didn't mind the wait; she'd been hoping for months to get the chance to speak with Princess Kelly, to show that she had what it took to join the cast of *The Real Baddies of Chicago*, and though she'd overheard someone saying that Princess, angry with Markio over something, had left the premises about an hour ago, Kitty was still going to meet with Markio, an urban fiction novelist of some renown with a movie of his own showing in theaters nationwide. Maybe she'd be able to talk him into putting a bug in Princess ear, or even- God willing – get him to assist her in the production of her horror film.

The sky's the limit.

Besides Kitty Jae, there were eleven other women gathered inside the luxury car garage, and Kitty wasn't the least bit surprised to see that Blicky Nicky was one of them. It was a huge, low slung building with stark white walls and white marble flooring. All twenty of the snow-white foreign vehicles— seven Rolls Royces, two Bugatti Veyrons, Four Lamborghinis, a Mercedes-Maybach S 680 4Matic, a Maserati coupe, two Aston Martins, a Mclaren, a Bentley Flying Spur, and an S Class Mercedes- Benz- were boxed in by brushed steel posts with black ribbons strung between them like crime scene tape. Kitty Jae had never seen a garage with it's own bathroom, but this one had one. There was also a refrigerator at the back wall that was filled to the top with gold bottles of Armond de Brignac a.k.a. Ace of Spades champagne.

Jessica Mensa ventured out onto her front porch and trained her camera first upon the wreckage of her Kia sedan, which lay crushed beneath an overturned Escalade.

"Oh my fuckin' God," the girl murmured in disbelief. "That whole truck done flipped over onto my car." As if the SUV had come to life and made a conscientious decision to tumble over onto *her* vehicle.

She panned the camera left and right, showing the other cars and trucks that had been knocked askew in the blast, and then she settled on the cratered redbrick building across the street. The building or what was left of it- was a blazing inferno, there were dollars of every denomination raining down from the sky, and just about every vehicle on the block had an alarm screaming out in a cacophony of earsplitting *beep-beep-beeps.*

"Aw, shit," Apple said, shaking his head. "Lord finna lose it."

Kitty Jae turned to look at the pudgy brown man. So did Jah. But Apple didn't say another word. Not that he needed to. He handed his KFC bucket to a girl Kitty didn't know and went hurrying off in the direction of the door that led to the mansion, and Kitty knew right then that the raining dollars belonged to Millionaire Markio. She'd heard rumors that Markio was plugged in with some drug cartel out of Mexico. And that he was the reason there was never a drought on drugs in the Lawndale neighborhood. Markio was from 15th and Trumbull, and the house that had apparently just been blown to smithereens was on 15th and Trumbull. It didn't take a rocket scientist to put two and two together.

Although Kitty had lived her whole life in North Lawndale – 16th and Millard just one block south and a few blocks west of the blast site, she had no idea who lived in the now gutted Trumbull Avenue home until Jah said it out loud.

"Ay, y'all," he announced to his fellow gang members. "Rev's house just blew up. On bro. I don't know if it was a gas leak or what, but that mufucka blew *up*!"

"Rev the barber?" Kitty Jae asked, and when Jah nodded yes, she said, "Daamn I hope he's okay. He just cut my son's hair this past Monday."

An unfamiliar voice said, "He just faded me up earlier today."

Kitty Jae turned toward the voice just as the man was approaching her. He bore a striking resemblance to Millionaire Markio: short, stocky, light skinned. He even had waves in his hair like Markio. But the similarities ended there. Where Markio was handsome, this much younger man was not. His front teeth were spread out like a spades hand, his nose was obscenely bulbous, and his left eye was cocked way over to the side while his right eye looked at her straight on.

"You dat stripper from Queen of Diamonds," he said licking his lips like a lizard. "I follow you on the Gram, comment on your pictures all the time. I'm Lil Archie from of Central Park."

And you should've stayed over there, Kitty thought but didn't say. Everyone inside the garage had arrived in cars and trucks that were parked in the wide driveway outside the garage. And Kitt had seen Lil Archie climb out of a BMW sedan with two girls and a guy named Chris that Kitty knew from around the way.

"Well, it was nice to meet you," Kitty Jae lied. "Stop by the club some time. Private dances are only fifty dollars per song."

"Yeah? And you'll give me one?"

"For fifty dollars."

"What if I ain't got the fifty dat night?"

"Then you won't get the private dance that night. Lap dances are cheaper. Just twenty dollars. I'm sure you can afford that."

"You got a man?"

"I do," she said, short and sweet like a marriage vow.

"Can you follow me back on the Insta?"

"I can't. Sorry I only follow people I know."

"But you follow Bryson Tiller. You follow Chief Keef."

"I know them." The lie sounded so funny coming out of her mouth that she almost laughed right in front of the man she had told it to. She saw her boyfriend rising to his feet behind Lil Archie and kept a neutral look on her face to keep Anton from spazzing out on the much smaller man. Anton who was also called Two Ton because he was so fucking huge.

Kitty Jae was still studying Lil Archie's hideous visage, wondering if they had ever been a women, dead or alive, who could look at him with honest eyes and call him an attractive man, when the first crack of gunfire knocked the thought from her mind.

She flinched, her shoulders jerking upward, her head dipping low. The other fourteen men and eleven women in the garage reacted in similar fashion, and Anton's right arm flew around behind his back, as if he was trying to throw a knockout punch at someone standing behind him.

A second gunshot sounded two seconds later, just as Kitty Jae gaze resettled on Archie's face. The left side of his head caved inward as if a sinkhole had suddenly appeared in his scalp, and the right side of his head came off in a visceral spray of brains, blood, and skull fragments. His left eye rolled toward Kitty Jae, and for one split second he was not cockeyed. Then his knees buckled. He swayed on his feet and went down.

Kitty Jae ducked and ran for the door Apple had gone through a moment earlier, wiping blood and brain matter from her face as she went, her heart a pounding reggae drum in her chest.

Chapter 13

He was no whipper snapper; his vision was nowhere near what it was fifty or sixty years ago. Yet and still, he was sure he'd hit his target. Absolutely sure of it. He'd missed that first shot, but the be next one, seen through his Leupold VX-1 rifle scope, which made his Winchester .300 bolt action capable of hitting a target at two thousand yards, was a direct hit.

"*Jackpot!*" Herb exclaimed, pumping a fist in the air. "Close that casket, baby!"

He was at the opening of Millionaire Markio's driveway, approximately one hundred yards out from the garage party he'd just nipped in the bud. He stored his high-powered rifle in the open trunk of his Hertz rental and then began the laborious task of disassembling the tripod he'd mounted his Winnie on before taking aim and giving old Markio one upside the noggin. He moved swiftly, but not all *that* swiftly; in rich neighborhoods like this one, where the obscenely wealthy resided in the luxurious comfort of their apartment complex-sized estates, the neighbors were rarely home. They were jet-setters, in the air more often than they were on land. And the garage partygoers were unlikely to come speeding off in his direction, since he'd fired at them from outside the garage, through the large squarish panes of glass in the garage door shutters.

"See ya later, alligators," Herb said, beaming a toothy smile as he stowed the tripod next to his rifle and closed the trunk on his rental car. It was a dark colored Honda he'd selected because there were *so many* of the godawful things on the streets of Chicago. There was no way the piggies could keep tags on all of them.

Nonetheless, he could never be too careful.

"That one was for you, Baby Stone," Herb said. He slipped in behind the wheel, grimacing against the pain of an underarm muscle he'd strained reaching up for the trunk lid.

"And now onto The Weasel."

Chapter 14

"So, Princess, tell us what happened."

Princess set down her phone and considered Thick Doll's opening gambit. "Last night," she began. "I got way too wasted at Queen A's All White party, threw up on my dress and everything, really embarrassed myself. Alexus had her personal bodyguard take me home to Markio's place in Lincoln Park, as you all know, that's where he, my daughter and I have been staying while my house I bought with Kamari is being renovated. Anyway, I figured I'd find Markio in his study, since he's been in there a lot lately, writing the script for his next movie. So, I brushed my teeth, checked on my baby, and then walked down the hall to his study with my mindset on getting him right as soon as I get there, and what do I see when I hit the doorway?"

"Kamari," Aqua said, because she knew.

"Kamari," Princess confirmed, with a twisted bounce of her head. "My own fucking sister. The bitch was sitting on his lap, and he had his hand all up in between her legs, rubbin' all on her pussy."

There was a collective gasp from the other seven women whom Princess Kelly had invited into her personal business. They were all seated around one end of the sixteen seat Honduran mahogany dining table in Aqua's dining room: Aqua, Thick Doll, Kimmy Kakes, Shmoney Rose, Cherish Taylor, Bunny Xxx and Sasha the Stallion—the full cast of The Real Baddies of Chicago.

And the MTN cameras were rolling.

"That dirty motherfucker," Kimmy Kakes said.

"Girl, which one?" Aqua chimed in "Because Kamari is just as guilty, if you ask me. All the men in the world, and she goes and chooses the one who's with her sister. I mean how low can you go?"

"All the way to the floor, apparently." This was Cherish Taylor, an exceedingly beautiful redbone of Brazilian and African American ancestry. She had long dark hair, sneaky gray eyes, high cheekbones, and the kind of natural curves most of the women in their group had paid damn good money for. Prinny had loathed the boujie bitch at first but Cherish had earned her respect after the on camera brawl that had started between Princess and Bunny and ended with most the cast on the floor kicking and screaming and pulling hair.

"Have you talked to either of them since you caught them together?"

Princess shook her head no. "But I called and left a voicemail for Kamari's boyfriend. Sent him a looong text message, too. I bet he called her not even twenty minutes after I left." She balled her hands into fist and sneered. Fighting back tears that went rolling down her cheeks anyway. "Karma's a baaaad bitch, though. Just know that."

"It really is," Aqua concurred. "I mean, look at what happened after you left. Two people got shot inside his garage, and one them died. On the news, they said the shooter might have fired some kind of sniper rifle from way down by the gate at the end his driveway!"

"Don't forget about that bombing!" Shmoney Rose cheerfully exhorted, in a singing voice that instantly reminded Princess of just how irritating she could be. "Somebody set off a bomb on 15th and Trumbull, and that's where he's from. That ain't no cowinkydink. He pissed somebody off, and whoever it is ain't fuckin around."

"None of this should be on camera," Thick Doll muttered in a near whisper. She was slumped back in her chair with her head down, her eyes on her hands in her lap, and her bottom lip stuck out in from of the top one. Everyone turned to her, waiting for her to go on. But she didn't speak again.

"He's definitely wrong for cheating on you with your sister," Kimmy Kakes said. She too was a gorgeous redbone, like Shmoney Rose, and the motherly voice of reason when the girls needed it most. "There's really no disputing that. But I wouldn't call what happened in that garage Karma, because Karma ain't that sinister. That was hate. Evil. And for all we know that bomb might've had nothing to do with him. He's from over there, but that's a ghetto, and that man is rich. He probably ain't seen these streets in years."

"I call bullshit," Shmoney said brusquely. "They're saying on the news that, that house on Trumbull was filled with money, like a goddam *Brinks* truck! Millions of dollars in cash, all burned up on the ground and blown to high hell. Markio broke our sister's heart, so I say we figure out how he's tied to this shit and turn it over to the F.B. Fucking I. *Snitch* on his bitch ass. Who wit' me?"

Cherish Taylor and Sasha the Stallion started laughing. Aqua, Bunny and Kimmy held their laughter in, but it was clear from their eyes and the reddening of their cheeks that they were dying to let it out, which happened when Bunny XXX got up, went to one of the three MTN cameramen, and with her sexy caramel brown face no more than six inches from the camera lens, said, "For the record I have no ties to this crazy bitch Shmoney Rose. I am not interested in snitching on anybody and I have nothing but love for any person she snitches on in the near or distant future."

They all laughed then. All except for Princess, who did find the situation humorous enough to warrant at least a couple insouciant chuckles, and Thick Doll, who got up from the table and left the room snatching the mic out of her beige

Prada sweater as Mike the cameraman, a wiry black man in his early forties, went rushing out behind her.

"What?" Shmoney yelled after Thick Doll. "What, snitches ain't cool no more? I just saw you on IG the other day, ridin' around listening to Gunna, and that nigga snitched on Thugga!"

Princess more than understood Thick Doll's reluctance to join in on the tomfoolery. Millionaire Markio really was a high-ranking gang member and also a drug kingpin with direct ties to Mexico's notorious Matamoros drug cartel. There was also a widespread belief that Markio had ordered Jesse "Baby Stone" Harris murder, and the belief alone had led to a significant increase in Chicago's murder rate. Speaking of such a man on a reality TV show that was watched by Forty to Fifty million viewers per week wasn't a wise idea. Especially not when the topic involved murder and the unsolved bombing of a stash house that had contained millions of dollars in drug money. Princess, who'd grown up around Baby Stone and had a daughter by Veemo, his right-hand man had lost a lot of friends over her decision to stick it out with Markio. Her own mother had advised her against it. Thick Doll's son was Baby Stone's namesake, his junior, and she made no attempt at hiding her contempt for Prinny's boyfriend of the last eleven months.

Ex-boyfriend, she reminded herself.

And right about now, as Princess sat looking over an eleven o'clock brunch of T-bone steak, cheese eggs, and buttery grits, thumbing tears from her eyes and doing her best to smile through the heartache, she found herself wishing that whoever had fired that death shot through the side of Archibald Wilson's head had instead done it to Markio Earl. The cheating bastard.

Everyone at the table was dressed for the snow that had now melted away. Princess had her own bedroom just up the hallway from Aqua's and she'd left a few outfits in the closet over the past couple of months. Perhaps to represent her gloomy disposition, Prinny had opted for a black Givenchy sweatsuit and heavy black Balenciaga boots. No jewelry, Minimal cosmetics. She wanted the audience to really experience her pain. Damn right she was exploiting her own miserable heartbreak for financial gain; as Alexus had told her time and again. "It's all about the ratings, bitch."

Shmoney's histrionics continued. "Fuck Markio. Ol' west side ass nigga. I never liked his punk ass books anyway. If I was you Prinny, I'd go back that mansion, walk in his closet, pick out his most expensive pair of shoes, and take a steaming hot dog diarrhea shit right in them bitches. Then pick 'em up and throw 'em right in his goddamn face. Let him feel what its like to be shitted on."

Cherish threw her head sideways and howled with laughter. A snot bubble blossomed from Aqua's left nostril as she laughed, and Kimmy pointed it out, eliciting a more raucous laughter that even Prinny couldn't help joining in on.

The moment ended with the girls getting up and surrounding Princess with a flurry of warm hugs and supportive exhortations that comforted her very soul. Some of it might have been done purely for the sake of the cameras, or to console the boss bitch producer who signed their paychecks, but the loving show of support still moved Princess to tears. It was a memorable moment she knew she'd never forget. What Black Girl Magic was all about.

Afterward, when the film crew and most of the cast left to film other segments for the show- Thick Doll's cemetery visit, which would be filled with drama, thanks in part to the $10,000 Princess had offered the mother of Baby Stone's other two children to pick a fight with her longtime adversary. A real-deal argument between Shmoney Rose and her current beau, a struggling actor with an apparent side chick and a serious knack for spending Shmoney's money. Princess retired to the bedroom Aqua had bestowed to her and sat cross legged in bed with her eyes rising to look at the

ABC 7News on her wall mounted flatscreen and falling to look at the phone she had in her hands.

Her five-year-old daughter, Vee, clad in a thick blue pajama set imprinted with images of Mickey and Minnie Mouse, kneeled beside her with her own iPhone in hand. Vee had paid for the phone herself, using the money she'd fished out of her cash stuffed piggy bank— hundreds, fifties, and twenties that looked eerily similar to the ones that kept going missing from the wallet in Prinny's purse.

On the TV, ABC anchorwoman, Val Warner, also a co-host on *Windy City Live!,* a program Prinny's mother could not go a day without watching was somber as she told of the "unspeakable tragedy" that had taken place at the Lincoln Park home of the "acclaimed author" Millionaire Markio. A video clip followed, showing the open front gates at the front of Markio's driveway. Yellow CRIME SCENE DO NOT CROSS tape stretched between the two redbrick pillars that buttressed the two wrought iron gates. The camera zoomed in on two bullet holes in the webbed pane of one garage door shutter. One of the shutters had been raised, and Princess could see tiny specks of blood spatter on the rear quarter panel of her beloved Maybach.

"Mommy, is Markio going to jail? Like my daddy." Vee pointed at the TV." Because the police are there, and police take people to jail, don't they? Hm? Huh, Mommy?"

I wish they'd take his punk ass to jail, Princess thought and instantly regretted. "No, I don't think Markio going to jail. Somebody hurt at his house, that's all. It happened after we came here to Auntie Aqua's house."

"I'm glad he's not going to jail, because, because a lot of my toys are over there, and the police, they might take my toys to jail, and bad people might *steal* them."

"Nobody wants your toys."

Vee's eyebrows went up. "Uh huhh. Gramma Joy said they got thiefs in jail, and they steal anything they can get their hands on."

"Yeah, but they wouldn't steal *your* toys. You got stinky toys."

"Hey!" Vee furrowed her brow. "My toys don't stink!"

"Yes, they do. Because you touch them with your stinky little *hands*, and your stinky little *fingers*."

Vee brought one hand up to her nose and gave the palm a meaningful sniff. Then, regarding her mother through squinted eyelids, she said. "My hands don't stink. You're crazy, mommy." She sat back on her heels and continued playing *Roblox* on her phone.

Princess had new text messages from twenty-nine of her fifty-six saved contacts. Most of them were family members and close friends who had seen the news and knew she'd been staying with Markio at the House of Lords while her and Kamari's Highland Park mansion was under renovations. Lost somewhere in the heavenly iClouds above were the hundreds of other phone numbers she'd accumulated over the years. Contacts she'd dumped like an overflowing ashtray shortly after the launch of her reality show, when it seemed like every person she'd ever met had started calling and texting with excited congratulations. That always led down a rocky road of absurd requests for financial assistance. Princess had a good heart, but she was nobody's sucker. It wasn't long before she'd changed her number and started deleting. As far as she was concerned every contact in that iCloud could stay there until hell froze over. They were as dead to her as Archibald Wilson was to the world at large.

Her mother, Joya, had texted her a few minutes ago. Even thought they'd already spoken at around seven his morning, when Prinny had got up to pee.

Leave it in God's hands, read the text. *And send me some money.*

Get it from God's hands, Prinny texted back, adding a prayer hands emoji for good measure.

Recently divorced, Joya was relaxing her bones at a lakefront Ritz-Carlton resort in Reynolds Lake Oconee, a private waterfront community just east of Atlanta. She was shacked up with some musclebound ex-con out of Baltimore who she'd met on Facebook. The Bird's Eye suite she'd so pompously chosen, and all its exorbitant room service fees were being charged to Prinny's credit card, costing her around a thousand dollars per day, but Princess didn't mind the ungodly expense. Money was no longer an issue. Princess only paid her Real Baddies cast members a little over three hundred thousand dollars per season, and that was separate from the funds the network allocated to pay the cast, the film crew, and a hundred other necessary expenses.

Joya replied with a string of laughing emojis, and Princess, smiling, sent her dear momma $2500 through Cash App.

A text from Grind read, *CALL ME ASAP!* Thinking it over, Princess glanced up at the flatscreen. The beautiful anchorwoman was talking about the Trumbull Avenue bombing. It cut to the first daylight images of the gutted building. A structure that might have been two or three stories tall when the day began but was now just an empty shell of rubble. Some of the men and women on the scene were members of the Chicago Police Department, but there were a lot of federal agents, as well, identified by the bold yellow letters stenciled onto their navy-blue windbreakers. ATF and FBI hoped a ring doorbell camera from across the street had captured the suspects on video, planting the bomb on a concrete porch that was no longer there. The suspects had yet to be identified, but it looked like a woman in an AT&T uniform wearing gloves and some sort of mask. There was also video of the explosion, with sound. The suspect vehicle was a white commercial van with Wisconsin plates.

Fearing that the bombing and maybe even the shooting at the House of Lords might possibly be related to the Hobos threat Grind and Big Gabby had warned her about— one of the new text messages had been from Big Gabby, telling Prinny about the skinny man who'd assaulted a Prime Shirt dancer for not knowing her whereabouts— Princess went ahead and dialed Grind's number.

"Hello?" Grind answered, after just half a ring.

"Hey. You asked me to call."

"I need my bread, on Larry. That's the only reason I asked you to call me. I'm out here really fucked up, ain't even got no pipe on me and I got fifty, sixty niggas who wanna kill me."

"Your backpack is at my place in Highland Park, but I'm not there right now. I can Cash App you the money, if you want it that way. Or I can wire it to your bank."

"Just shoot me five or six thousand until you can get to my bookbag, 'cause I need my pole outta there, too. That Glock."

"Why don't you just buy yourself one with the money I'm about to send you?"

"That's what I'ma do. Still need that one. I don't think you fully understand the... Damn, wait a minute. It's a word for..."

"Gravity?" Princess offered.

"That's it. You don't understand that gravity. The Hobos ain't no regular organization. They got GDs, BDs, Four Corner Hustlers, Mickey Cobras. Four or five different gangs all working together. As much as I hate to say it, I'm actual kinda glad you got ol' boy behind you. Ain't too many niggas gon' be bold enough to cross them Vice Lords."

"Me and ol' boy ain't together no more," Prinny said bitterly, just as Vee dropped her phone, hopped down off the lovely spacious bed and went tattering off toward the adjoining bathroom. Princes shouted after her. "Don't forget to wash those stinky hands!" Then to Grind, she said, "I caught him with my sister on his fucking lap last night."

And as she spoke, Vee shouted back. "I *always* wash my hands! It's why they smell like *soap*, silly." The beads at the ends of her braids clacked together as she ran, reminding Princess of the sound Markio's diamond chain made when he walked, or when they wrestled playfully in bed, or when he was kneeling behind her, fucking her deeper and better than any man she'd ever been intimate with.

Fresh tears welled up in her eyes. She picked up a tissue from the Kleenex box on her nightstand and wiped them away.

"Goddamn you, Markio. Damn you to hell."

"It could've been innocent," Grind suggested optimistically.

"He was rubbing her fucking pussy!"

"Oh Damn. Sorry to hear dat, G. On gang, I ain't... damn."

"I know, right? And they haven't even called me since that shit happened. No calls, no texts from Markio. I mean, I understand that somebody ended up getting killed in his garage right after I left, and I can see how that might've thrown them both off a little, but still. No calls? Not even a text message?"

For a long moment, Grind said nothing. Prinny heard rap music in the background. She knew the rappers name, but she couldn't quite remember the adjective that came before it. He was either Lil Pappy or Young Pappy, and one thing Princess did know about him was that he was dead, killed in a barrage of gunfire like the countless other Chicago rappers who came before him. Prinny listened.

"...I wish a nigga would try to run up on Pap. Hell yeah, I can fight, but I rather up strap I'll rather up pole on a nigga, gotta keep a pole on me, nigga I'm too known for a nigga, how you get caught wit a pole, lil nigga and you home already, Lord knows yo done told on a nigga..."

Grind said, "Don't take this the wrong way, but that whole situation couldn't been avoided had you kept your sister away from your man."

Prinny's jaw dropped. "Are you serious? Are you seriously blaming this on me?"

"Just listen. Hear me out. You seen Players Club, right? With Lisa Raye? Remember when her thick ass sister was in that kitchen in her panties, and buddy who played Lisa Raye's boyfriend was watching her? Next thing you know he had her butt bootyhole naked fucking the shit out of her."

This nigga can't be serious. "Grind, are you hearing yourself?"

"Hold on, gang. I just want you to think of Kamari for a second. Tall chocolate, thick as fuck, pretty as fuck. She might be your lil sister but that's a grown woman. I saw on Instagram that she got a man, that boxer nigga, but he prob'ly ain't been boxing that pussy how she want him to. Led her right to ya guy."

Princess stretched her legs out in front of her and studied her toenails, thinking not of the pedicure she felt she needed but of the truly plausible theory Grind had just put forth. It was true that Kamari was a remarkably gorgeous young woman, with more curves than a Nascar racetrack. It was also true that Kamari's boyfriend was an abject failure in the sex department; she had told Princess all about Malcom's many short comings, emphasis on the short. Prinny could not even count the number of times she'd bragged to Kamari about Markio's dick size, and about how long he could last in bed.

(*Hours, Kamari, Literally hours.*")

Had her own fat mouth been the catalyst for what she'd walked in on last night? She didn't want to think about it.

"The Hobo's came looking for me at QOD," she said fingering a lock of her hair from her forehead. "Some boy name Paris. They say he grabbed Kitty Jae- some new Prime Time Girl- and asked her where I was at."

"See? I told you. That's why I told you to watch out. He used to be kinda stocky, but I shot him up when they tried to rob me. And I guess he lost some weight behind that. Listen,

125

that man is *dangerous*. I mean that in every sense of the word. You need to take some kinda precautions. Hire some security. Call them Stones you grew up with and get them to hawk buddy ass down. You need to drop a bag on his head and get him knocked off before he can get to you, 'cause he ain't gon' stop. You saw what they tried to do to me the last time I got out the county."

"I did see. And I killed both of 'em."

"That's 'cause they weren't focused on you. They came for me that time and don't get me wrong, I thank you for that; you save my life that day but it'll be different when they come for you. They know you got good aim and they know you got good money. They gon' pop out on you in broad daylight and blitz yo' lul ass, on Larry. Same way them O Block niggas did FBG Duck. I'm tellin' you what's real. You better drop that bag, on Paris, on Bowlegs—on all dem niggas. The one advantage you got is that money. I'd advise you to use it."

Princess heaved a breath, chewing the corner of her bottom lip. The toilet in her bathroom flushed. Her chair she'd put in there solely for Vee's use, went sliding across the floor. Five seconds later the faucet came on.

"Do you think the Hobos were behind that bombing," she asked. "And that shooting at Markio's mansion?"

Grind didn't even hesitate. "Nope. Not a chance."

"And why do you say that?"

"Because its common fuckin' sense. CNN said the shooter was a hundred yards away when he shot into that garage. A hundred… yards .. away. Name one street nigga you know who can do some shit like that. You can't. That was some Jason Bourne type shit. My lil brother just showed me this video they got floating around on social media. It's the nigga Archie who got killed in that garage, but from the side, the boy looks just like Millionaire Markio. I think he got killed for that very reason. Mistaken identity."

Another plausible theory. Grind was on a roll.

"And what about the bomb?" Prinny asked.

"Proves my point even further. Hobos don't use bombs, they use guns. Handguns, shotguns, and machine guns. I don't think it's no kinda coincidence that somebody planted a bomb on his block around the same time some sniper shot into his garage from a football field away. That right there." He whistled. "I don't even know. Me and you only got the Hobos to worry about, and that's dangerous enough, but what *Markio* got goin' on? I ain't gon' lie, that nigga might need the Secret Service to keep him alive. Somebody's on his ass, and whoever it is, he's a lot more dangerous than the Hobos."

The ominous words sent a wintry chill down Princess spine. Had she literally dodged a bullet leaving Markio when she had? Was Kamari in some kind of danger? It was improbable that the House of Lords shooting and the Trumbull Avenue bombing weren't connected, especially since they transpired within minutes of each other.

Vee came padding out of the bathroom, sniffing the palms of her hands, her bright eyes aglow with the natural innocence of childhood.

"Send me your Cash App information so I can send you this money. Get yourself somewhere safe, a hotel suite downtown somewhere and call me when you get there so I know you're okay."

"A'ight. You be safe too. And since you and Markio ain't together no more, maybe we can—"

Princess ended the call right then, She gave Vee a hand in climbing back onto the bed, and when she received the Cash App info from Grind she sent him $9000. More than enough for him to buy himself a decent handgun, a few nice outfits, and a really nice hotel room he could lay low in until he figured out his next move.

As for her own next move, Prinny had just one phone number in mind.

She picked up her phone and dialed it.

Chapter 15

The more she tried not to think about it, the more it kept flashing in front of her eyes. Archie's repulsively formed face, the reptilian lick of his lips, the melancholy in his forward-facing right eye when it finally registered that he had absolutely no chance with the impossibly beautiful exotic dancer he'd probably been beating off to for the past several months.

And then POW! His head sinking in on the left side, that lazy left eye spinning forward as if taking the place of the right eye that had just been blown clear out of its socket.

Even worse was what she'd tasted: blood and bone and brains, hot and wet in her mouth, the latter rolling along her teeth and gums until she'd paused to spit it out and vomit on the tessellated marble floor in the high ceiling foyer of Millionaire Markio's sprawling gray stone fortress. A few frightened runners slipped in her fetid spew and landed on their asses and elbows.

Such traumatizing memories.

Kitty Jae opened her eyes and peeled her forehead off the glass of the vending machine she'd been leaning forward against. She signed and peered in at the refrigerated comestibles. There were plastic wrapped sandwiches up top— chicken, fish, beef, pork— and toward the bottom there were pies and cakes of a wide variety, individuals slices meant for the individual consumer.

"Ma, are you okay?"

It was Omar, her ten-year-old, standing at the next vending machine over, the one with all the bags of potato chips and packets of candy trapped behind coils of gray metal. His olive-colored eyes were fixed on the rows of snacks in front of him, but apparently his peripheral vision was working just fine.

Kitty Jae turned right away to tell him a bold-faced lie, to say she was doing just great, that everything was peaches and he should focus on which snack he wanted to munch on and leave his dear Ma to her thoughts, but when she opened her mouth, the truth came tumbling right out- like a rubber chuck of brain matter rolling off the tongue.

"No, Omar I'm not alright," she said hugging herself. "I'm so far from okay right now it don't make sense."

"Doesn't make sense," he corrected.

"Boy, don't make me slap you in front of these white people." His notable handsome face pressed into an immensely handsome smile. He stepped up punched in a letter and number and watched the coil in a line of ranch flavored Doritos begin it's slow roll forward.

"Two Ton gon' be aight," he said using Anton's nickname. "That doctor said he'll live, and that's what's important, Ma. It's not the end of the world. Watch, when he comes out of that second surgery, and comes down off whatever anesthetics they used to numb the pain, he'll be the same old Two Ton. Watch and see."

Kitty's view was less sanguine. The high-powered rifle slug had come very close to blowing the lower half of Anton's right arm completely off, and Dr. Geary, a bespectacled man in his mid to late sixties who was very thin and almost bald, his skin sallow and sagging had informed her that the arm would need to be amputated below the elbow. What was Anton going to do with one arm? Direct traffic?

"Where'd you learn a word like anesthetics?" Kitty asked, to keep herself from mentioning Lil Archie's exploding head. "I didn't learn that word until I was right here in this hospital having you."

"*Call of Duty*," Omar replied and nothing more.

Kitty Jae selected a spicy chicken sandwich and an apple pie, and from the beverage machine she purchased an Evian water for herself and a Mountain Dew for Omar.

They were in a carpeted waiting area just down the hall from Anton's assigned room. The seats and backrests of the chairs that lined the east and north walls were made of thick, beveled, burgundy fence.

Omar –or OJ, as he was sometimes called—picked a chair and sat to enjoy his pop and chips, while Kitty Jae warmed her sandwich at the microwave and stared up at the muted television that was bolted high up on a south wall. It was turned to channel seven. That gorgeous, brown-skinned anchorwoman, with her short dark hair and big contagious smile, was speaking with a retired FBI special agent about the House of Lords shooting suspect's behavioral profile, and the possible connection to the Trumbull Avenue bombing.

"Ma, that's my woman crush," Omar announced brightly. "Val Warner." He uttered the name yearningly. "She so fiiine, man, man, *man!*" He snickered and crunched down on a triangular yellow chip.

Kitty rolled her eyes, shook her head, and turned back to the microwave, holding her elbows in both hands. The intense ache in her wrist had faded to a distant throb. The police had taken her Gucci sweatshirt for evidence, so she'd had Omar get the red Celine hoodie she now wore out of her drawer before his crazy Aunt Shalonda brought him up to the hospital where he'd taken his very first breaths. Northwestern Memorial.

She'd set the Hostess apple pie atop the microwave, and now, looking at the Cinnamon-drizzled guts oozing out of the crust in the advertised image on the package, she suddenly realized that the sugary little clumps of apple would feel similar to the bits of brain she'd come sickeningly close to swallowing.

She hugged herself and shivered. Two female nurses went scurrying past in the hallway, which branched off both directions like a capital-L. They both wore their hair in buoyant ponytails that bounced as they walked and talked, their conversation centered round their unfounded belief that Islamic extremist were obviously responsible for the Trumbull Avenue bombing.

"It's all those immigrants Biden let into the country," the blonde conjectured. "Syrian, Libyans, Fucking *Iraqis*'. Mad that guys like that Markio feller can get filthy rich here in America while they blow each other up in the Middle East."

"More like that Middle Beast!" quipped the brunette. "You ask me, I say they're pissed at Alexus. You know she and Bulletface used to live on Trumbull Avenue and they're close with Millionaire Markio. You know those Muslim, the ones over there, they hate it when a woman has power, and Alexus is the richest bitch on the fucking planet! Take that Osama...."

Their voices faded away. So did the steady whap of their Crocs on the spotless linoleum tiled floor.

"OJ, if you want this apple pie, you can have it," Kitty said, not even wanting to look at the thing anymore.

"Sure, I'll take it." He was on his feet a second later, marching over in his Jordan sneakers, stonewashed jeans, and gray Amiri tee. "You know I'm tryin' to get my muscles up. Need all the calories I can get. Got two girlfriends and one on the way."

The microwave dinged and Kitty's cell phone rang simultaneously. She picked the steaming sandwich out of the microwave and left Omar to warm his pie as she headed back up the hallway toward Anton's room, taking her ringing phone from her back pocket. It was Big Gabby, probably calling to see if Kitty was going to make it in. Blabbermouth

Blicky had probably called Gabby and told her everything; Kitty didn't even need to answer the call to know that.

Turning into the open door of Anton's hospital room, Kitty Jae hurried to her leatherette armchair, so she could answer the call before it went to voicemail. She was lowering her ample bottom to the seat when she heard a voice that made her forget all about the call.

"The Weasel's no fun."

Herb's raspy voice bottomed out in a tobacco-torn whisper that made the hairs on the back of Kitty's neck stand on end.

She looked up and spotted him instantly. The old man was standing across the room from her. In the place where Anton's bed had been before it was rolled out of the room with him on it less than twenty minutes ago. He donned a suit and tie of varying shades of green, and he was leaning forward on a gleaming wooden cane, with one hand clasped over the other. Add to that his top hat and feather, and the octogenarian was like a mobster right out of the 1930's.

"How did you get in here?" Kitty asked, it was the only question that came to mind.

"Door was open," he said, and shrugged. "I walked in."

His scent was heavy in the room; Kitty hadn't smelled it when she entered the room, but she smelled it now. Cigarette smoke and antiquated cologne. The decaying stench of age.

"No, I'm saying how did you know I was *here*? That's what I'm asking. Who told you I was *here*?" The rising steam from the microwaveable bag her sandwich came prepacked in seared her knuckle. She turned and placed it on the windowsill behind her, narrowing her eyes at the glare of midday sunlight but keeping them transfixed on the deeply lined black face across the room from her.

"Heard it through the grapevine," he said, lifting his scrawny shoulders again. "Also, heard that your boy toy took a round through the arm. How's he faring?"

Kitty Jae's squint became even more narrow, regarding the enigmatic elder through razor slits, unconsciously rolling the wrist Paris the Hobo had squeezed.

"He's doing just fine." She told the lie through clenched teeth, glancing at the open doorway as an orderly stalked past pushing a rolling array of cleaning supplies." Why are you here? And where's that money you promised?"

"Well," Herb said, "since the answer to both questions is one and the same, let's just I came here to shoot two birds with one stone."

Kill two birds with one stone, Kitty Jae thought, but she didn't say it, because the old man lowered his head and laughed in a way that Kitty found uniquely disturbing.

Keck, keck, keck, keck, keck, it went. Like a car engine struggling to turn over. A vein appeared amid the many creases in his forehead. His head twisted left and right on his neck.

This old motherfucker is off his rocker, Kitty thought to herself or maybe it wasn't to herself. Maybe it was a shared thought, some sort of telepathy, because the old motherfucker commented on it.

"I know what you're thinking," he said, struggling to catch his breath. He knocked the rubber tipped base of his cane on the square of tile he stood on. "This old man's off his rocker, a few eggs short of a dozen, two whores short of a threesome."

Keck, keck, keck. He slapped his knee.

"But no. No, I assure you that's not the case. The old brain is in perfect working order. In the words of my old friend Jeff Fort, 'all's well.' I actually came here to give you your money. My girls have it for you down in the parking lot. We're parked right by that hot new set of wheels you went out and got. That G-Wagon."

After that the two of them didn't speak for a while. He made a come-hither motion with one leathering old hand and Kitty Jae got up to follow him out into the hallway. Cautious optimism- she'd heard of it in books and on television, but she'd never experienced it until now.

There was an elevator right outside the waiting area. Omar was sitting with his piping hot pie in one hand, flipping through channels with a TV remote he'd likely charmed some nurse in to giving him.

"Keep your narrow butt right there," Kitty said, pointing at Omar with the hand she held her phone in. "I'm going down to the parking lot for a minute."

"Whose grandaddy is that?" Omar turned on his smile. 'Two Ton ain't been here more than a couple hours and you've already found yourself a sugar daddy. Wait until I tell Two Ton."

Herbert Harris loosed a series of kecks, coughed twice, and used the bottom of his cane to press the elevator button. Kitty Jae was cranking up a middle finger in her son's direction when the doors parted in front of her.

Inside the elevator, silence prevailed. Mainly because there was a homely young male nurse in dark blue scrubs standing behind a wheelchair that held a morbidly obese woman of about fifty. The woman kept rummaging in her oversized faux leather purse. "Got a snickers bar hiding in her some doggone-where." The white woman grumbled.

Kitty Jae stifled a laugh and turned her attention to Herbert studying him out of the corner of her eye. He might have been ancient and peculiar, maybe even a little scary, but there was no denying his keen eye for fashion. His slick green suit was like something you'd see advertised in *GQ Magazine*- nothing like those gaudy green atrocities the Bishop Don "Magic" Juan was known to wear.

The elevator stopped on the fourth floor and the nurse wheeled his heavy load into the great labyrinth beyond.

When the doors slid shut in front of her, Kitty Jae said, "I need to know how you found me. In all seriousness. That's creeping me the fuck out."

"People talk."

134

"Blicky Nicky?"

"Is that what they call her?" *Keck, keck, keck.* "I knew it was Nicky something. I like that other Nicki. The rap girl."

"Oh my God, I can't *stand* that bitch."

"Who, the rap girl?"

"No. That's Nicki Minaj. I'm talking about Blicky Nicky, AKA *Blabbermouth Blicky.* What's *wrong* with that girl? Who'd she tell?"

"My nephew had a son with Karionna. Today's my nephew's birthday. I visited his gravesite a little while ago, and she showed up as I was leaving. We said a few words in passing, and when I stopped to get in a word with Little Jesse, I overheard Karionna's phone call with the Nicky girl. Nicky told her some guy got his noggin blown off right in front of you, and that your boyfriend got shot too. I read the *Sun-Times* everyday on my phone. An article I read about that shooting named the victim and said he was brought here, so I called the hospital and told them the Hicks guy was my son and that got me the room number. Easy like Sunday morning."

Kitty Jae closed her eyes and breathed. She had a growing list of vexations, and that ignorant hoe Blicky Nicky was racing to the top of the list. Fast.

When she opened her eyes, she was taken aback to see that Herb was looking at her with definite glee in his eyes. Tyra Banks had coined a name for that particular look. Smizing. Smiling with the eyes.

"What was it like, seeing that guy's noggin explode right before your eyes?" He turned his whole body to face her, and Kitty got the sense that he was watching for a reaction, that for some reason he was gravely interested in her answer to his sick, twisted questions. "And who do you think did it? Think it was the Hobos? Nicky told Karionna that you got snatched up by one of the Hobos?"

Kitty Jae raised her shoulders. "I didn't really see that boy get shot. I was too focused on my man. And who knows? It might've been the Hobos who did it, or it could've been some illegal immigrant from the Middle East. You never know."

The smiling eyes dimmed. "Hmm." his gaze returned back to the chrome sliding door, his posture ramrod straight, as if the cane were merely a prop.

They left the elevator on the ground floor and exited the building side by side, with Herb effortlessly matching her pace. His matte black Bentley Mulsanne sat next to her Mercedes Benz G-Wagon. The two women seated inside the Mulsanne climbed out when they saw Kitty and Herb draw nearer, popping the trunk and walking around to it. The girls were both dark in complexion and slender build, wearing identical pantsuits that were as black as their car and as expensive looking as Herb's fine threads.

Kitty Jae opened the rear storage compartment of her G-Wagon and watched as one of the girls lifted out the same black leather duffle bag that Kitty had looked into on that warm June morning, and when the girl dropped the duffle into Kitty's SUV, Kitty stepped forward and unzipped it to stare in at all those beautiful stacks of hundreds again. She moved them around, fanned through a couple of bundles and nodded her approval as a great flood of relief washed through her. *My movie*, she thought, her eyes filling with tears. *The bank loan. Lord Jesus, thank you!*

She wiped her eyes and turned to thank Herb, but he and his two dames were already driving away. Which was a good thing, an even greater relief. As far as Kitty Jae was concerned, she could go the rest of her life without ever laying eyes on that scary old man again.

She'd figured it out on the elevator ride down.

Herbert Harris was the House of Lord shooter, and one of those girls of his was the Trumbull Avenue bomber.

Chapter 16

"…So, you know, I was standin' way back by this big dumb ass refrigerator that was, like full of Ace of Spades champagne, and I do mean all-the-way-to-the top full. Wasn't even no shelves, just gold bottles laid sideways and piled from the floor of that refrigerator to the motherfuckin' roof. And that's on Big A. Oh, and I know it was Ace of Spades, too, and not just because I pop my pussy at your strip club most every night. My daddy used to own a liquor store. It was out in Bellwood, around the corner from that house Miss Daniels stayed in by the train tracks."

"Oh my fuckin' *Gaaawd*," said the gorgeous high yellow girl who was seated next to Weezy on his gargantuan dark blue sofa. Blicky couldn't quite remember the pretty bitch's name, but she liked the view of the fat yellow butt cheeks bulging out the back of those baby blue booty shorts.

"Bitch, I thought you said your daddy worked for the post office."

"He diiid. But then he retired from the post office and used his savings to open a liquor store. *Duhh.* Now will you shut up and let me talk? Because I can go home. I ain't go to put up with this disrespect."

"All you've been doin' is talking; and you ain't said nothin' yet."

Weezy raised his mildly deformed right hand to silence the pretty bitch. "Just let her talk, baby."

"Yeah, *baby*, just let me talk. Okay? Okay bitch? Muchas gracias. Muchas fuckin gracias." And with a muchas ghetto sway of her head, Blicky shifted her attention back to the owner of the incredibly spacious Sheraton Suites condo the three of them were now seated in. "As I was *sayin'*, I was standin' over by that big ass refrigerator, bouncing my lil cheeks to the Sicko Mode song somebody had playin', when all of a sudden POW!"

Blicky jumped in the giant blue easy chair she was perched on as if she'd been shot herself. "First thing I told them other bitches was bitch, that was a gunshot. Because I know gunshots when I hear 'em. I'm from Parkway Garden, O Block, you know, so I know all about gunshots. Plus, my daddy was a marksman, the best of the best, took me to the gun range all the time. So, I know all about gunshots."

"Fuck that," the pretty bitch said, and picked up her phone. "Tell me his name. I need to Google this nigga."

"Google deez nuts," Blicky said sourly, and turned back to the man in charge. "So, anyways, I see Kitty Jae's boyfriend, some big ass nigga they call Three Tons, or some shit like that. I see him go down with his forearm all blasted open. The next thing I know, this ugly cock eyed nigga who was standing right in front of Kitty Jae gets all his oodles and noodles blown clean out the side of his godddamn head."

"Did you happen to get a look at the shooter?" Weezy asked. He was dressed oddly to be indoors, in a navy blue bullet proof vest strapped over a black tee, black sweatpants, and black Timberland boots. Two Glock pistols lay on the coffee table in front of him. He sat forward, steepled his fingers and said. "I need you to think long and hard about that one. Did you look outside and see anybody out there?"

"Not at first, I didn't. I had to save that man first. I took off the T-shirt I had on under my hoodie and use it as a tourniquet

To stanch the bleeding." Blicky looked at the pretty bitch and smiled. "Learned that from my daddy too." Then back to Weezy. "But once I got his arm all wrapped, I did look out there to see if I could see anything. Everybody else ran into the mansion and there I was, standing there with Three Ton's blood all on my fucking clothes and on my face and even dripping from my fingers. Like I was lady Dracula or some shit. I went to the big white slide-up door and looked out through the bullet holes in the glass, and I did see something way down at the end of the driveway. Like right when you turn in."

"Yeah?" Weezy scooted forward some more. "And what was it? What did you see?"

A merry smile played at the corners of Blicky Nicky's mouth. The sight of Weezy sitting there on the edge of his seat, hanging onto her every word, brought a great well of delight to her chest. Blicky loved attention, absolutely craved it, and right now she was the woman of the hour.

"Okay sooo," she began. "There was this man. He was too far away for me to see any real details, but he was doing something behind this small car—I believed it was a Honda and I remember thinking to myself. Man, that guy moved like he's old or something. I thought to take a picture so I flung some of the blood off my fingers and wiped my hands on my ass, got some blood on that clean ass Maybach but oh well, you know. Shit happens. Anyway, by the time I got my phone out, the man was pulling off from the driveway, and Three Tons was crying like a little bitch, so I called 9-1-1 and told the dispatch lady we needed an ambulance. They showed up a minute or so later like they always do in rich white neighborhoods like they were parked right up the street somewhere. Paramedic guy said I saved Three Ton's life with that torniquet."

Weezy sat back and nodded his head, apparently having heard all he'd needed to hear. There was a Ziploc bag filled with melting ice cubes wrapped in a thick blue bath towel on the armrest next to him, and Blicky extrapolated that he had it there to treat the swelling on the side of his face, though he had yet to pick it up since she arrived twenty minutes earlier.

The pretty bitch had been turned sideways, with one leg folded under her and one hand on the nape of Weezy's neck, massaging the taut muscles with her pretty fingers. Now she turned to face forward, and Blicky saw that the pretty bitch looked a lot like Ice Spice.

Blicky said, "Bet you wish your daddy could've taught you that tourniquet trick, huh? Medics called me a lifesaver. I'm a hero, bitch. A motherfucking she-ro. Remember that Durk and Lil Baby album, *The Voice of Heros?* Well, guess what? I'm one of those voices?"

"I can't even take you serious."

"You should take me serious. 'Cause my daddy was a boxer, too, and he taught me every move. I'll punch those freckles right off your pretty little face."

The pretty bitch started to get up and for a fleeting second Blicky thought she'd talked herself into some action. She became jittery with real excitement, because if there was one thing she craved more than attention it was action, whether fussing, fighting or fornicating, she was all about the action.

But there was no action to be had; the pretty bitch just wasn't about it. She said, "I'll be in the bedroom when you get done with your company," kissed Weezy on the jaw, and headed off in her Fendi slippers, giving Blicky's chair a wide berth. Blicky leaned to the side and swiveled her head, watching the pretty bitch go.

"Did you talk to the po-leece about what you saw?" Weezy asked, twirling a finger in the hair of his beard.

"Boy, I don't talk to no po-leece, is you crazy? My daddy would kill me. I dialed 9-1-1 and specially asked for an ambulance, told that dispatcher I ain't see shit. I ain't never told on nobody." Blicky spun around in her seat, certain she'd find the pretty bitch creeping in for a sneak attack, but there was no one there. "In my life."

Weezy chuckled, "Baby ain't tryna fight you," he said, but he too was behaving nervously, tossing repeated glances at the towering blue curtain that sealed them in from the outside world.

"You never know," Blicky said, glancing back again. "People are sneaky. Look at how Amber Rose snuck up on my girl Joselyn Hernandez. Did you see that on College Hill? The Puerto Rican Princess never saw it coming. Just WHAM! Almost took her whole goddamn head off. By the way, what happened to your head? Looks like somebody punched you even harder than Amber hit Joselyn.

Weezy was opening his mouth to speak when Blicky raised a hand to stop him.

"Nevermind. Don't even know why I said that when I know the answer already. I talked to Gabby when I was getting dressed this morning, a girl can do two things at once, you know. Plus, I talked to her again when I was on my over here. She told me she had to kick you upside your mother fuckin' head for putting your hands on her. Said you tried to do her like ol' boy did Kitty Jae, twisted her wrist. Shame on you for that, Weezy. Like, for real, for real." She laughed, her eyes brightening with glee. "Tell you what, though. I didn't think the big bitch could kick that high! Shocked the shit outta you, didn't it?"

Weezy started laughing then. He laughed for quite a while, in fact, and Blicky laughed right along with him, because laughter was action, too, and that's what Blicky was all about.

"Do you ever turn down?"

"Turn *down*?" Blicky said as if she'd taken offense. "Turn down? Turn down for what? Nigga, I'm all about the turn up."

She felt compelled to prove it, so she jumped up, turned her back to Weezy, and vibrated her thighs in a way that made her fat ass shake and jiggle in her skintight Chanel body suit, which was purple like her six-inch Christian

Louboutin heels, her gel-manicured fingernails and her Fenty lipstick. She looked back at him with her tongue out and was elated to see him staring at her natural Puerto Rican humps.

After that she styled around the ornate coffee table an took the pretty bitch's seat. She kissed him on the jaw in roughly the same area the pretty bitch had kissed him. The Ice Spice wannabe. Fucking *Warm* Spice.

She said, "I was right, wasn't I? About it being an old man who shot into that garage. It's the same man who cut off your hand, ain't it? Only he's after Millionaire Markio now. Why's that?"

"I don't know. Goddamn, you ask a lot of fuckin' questions."

"Did you know that Millionaire Markio and Princess broke up last night? Sure did, this boy they call Gucci Ball recorded video of her going ape-shit on Markio in that garage, happened right before I got there. I tricked him into letting me send the video to my phone. I told him I wanted to put my number in his contacts, which I did do, but I also texted that video to my phone. Wanna see it? I'll show it to you."

"Just tell me what was on it."

"Oh, let me tell," Blicky said, dragging out the word tell for four whole seconds. "Princess walked in on Markio and *Kamari!* Her motherfuckin' sister! Can you believe that shit? I sent that video straight to TMZ. The Shade Room too, 'cause you know I been a TSR Roommate from day one. Princess gon' be pissed, because that's going viral, and I won't feel bad at all. And you wanna know why?"

Rubbing the palm of his good hand down his face, Weezy chuckled and said, "Not really but I'm sure you—"

"Because that BITCH should've put me on the show." Blicky glanced down the long hallway the pretty bitch had disappeared through, suddenly remembering the bitch's mocking tone. I can't even take you serious. The Fuck was that supposed to mean? Blicky thought, flickering her eyes back to Weezy. "You know what? I should suck your dick. Can I suck your dick?"

"If that'll shut you up, feel free."

She reached down into his sweats and wrestled out his member. It was a fat black thing, not much to it the way of length, but Blicky thought it might harden into something impressive. She smiled and bit her lower lip, jacking his dick in her hand, watching it fill out and lengthen. Then she turned to the vacant hallway and shouted.

"Hey Spice! I am about to gobble your man's dick and I'm swallowing the babies too. You can put the pregnancy dream on the back burner, *baby!*"

Warm Spice's reply was distant but clear: "Please, just put it in your mouth and keep it there."

Blicky did just that.

Chapter 17

The very clearly insane Puerto Rican girl who'd named herself Blicky Nicky sucked dick the same way she talked-fast and unceasingly. And it was good quality head, too; just two minutes in and already Weezy's breaths were hitching, almost like an old car engine struggling to come alive one last time.

Almost like the teeth clenching laugh that belonged to Herbert T Harris

Keck, keck, keck.

Weezy heard it now echoing somewhere in the dim recesses of his brain, loud and abrasive as the sound of a great black stallion galloping the halls of an abandoned school building – a red eyed fire breathing devil of a thoroughbred with steel hooves that shattered the tiled flooring to a billion pieces as it advanced forward.

Weezy hated Herbert T Harris with a furious passion.

Twenty-four years ago when Weezy was seventeen and his brother Jaems "Jay Folks" Sullivan was nineteen, he and Jay folks had walked out of a female friend's house on 64th and Carpenter, the two of them laughing discussing the train they'd just run on the girl, when a muddy gray '96 Impala SS had suddenly come lancing up the street in their direction. Weezy had recognized the car immediately; it was the same Chevy a rival set of Black Disciples had used in a drive by on his gang the previous week. Shoving Weezy into the gangway, Jay Folks had taken off running up the sidewalk…

just as someone in the passenger's seat of the Impala was shoving the long steel barrel of an AK-47 out his window to open fire. Weezy was halfway to the alley way when he heard the first soul-shaking claps of gunfire and he continued on across the alley way into the backyard of his cousin Flukey's house on Aberdeen, where two pistols lay in the bushes that ran along the rear of the home. More gunfire ensued. Weezy had rushed back to Carpenter Street and sent half dozen shots at that impala just as it went tearing off around the corner up the street. Near the end of the block, slumped backward over a short chain link fence with his chest shot to shreds and most of his head missing, was Jay Folks. The homicide had gone unsolved, and Weezy harbored a special hatred for his brother's unnamed killer – but even that hatred paled in comparison to the way he felt about Herbert T Harris.

Never in life had Weezy been so afraid to go outside. It was a beautiful day out there, but he was too fearful of a high-powered rifle slug through the skull to even consider opening a curtain. There were too many tall buildings on this particular stretch of Illinois Street, every window a potential sniper's nest.

And there was another first on the horizon, Weezy was actually contemplating making a call to the police, or maybe even to the FBI— a glaring red line he'd never even come close to crossing. But what choice did he have? The old man was like a shadow figure, a ghost that stood at the edge of your vision and then vanished when you turned to look at it head-on. Weezy had recently risen to the rank of Senior Regent, a status that gave him limitless control over a vast swaths of Gangster Disciple territory and hundreds of bloodthirsty young gunslingers, and yet he remained powerless against a man who was old enough to be his grandfather.

He winced as Blicky Nicky's teeth nicked the head of his dick. She squeezed his meat and worked her tongue, sucking hard. Looking down at her, Weezy thought she was one of the most beautiful girls to ever walk through the doors of his strip club. She had a small tattoo behind her left ear. A green stem topped with a purple rosebud. Today, she wore her long dark hair in pigtails, like a Chinese schoolgirl. Her waist was just twenty-three inches around, while her hip measurements doubled that.

Her lips, currently wet with a bubbly accumulation of saliva, were as full and sumptuous as Megan Goode's. Her eyes were a shimmery gray, shrewd and watchful, always darting around to take in everything at once. Even now, he saw her eyes at work, studying his twin Glocks on the table, and the rich upholstery of his sofa, and the light sprinkle of marijuana crumbs on the left knee of his black pyramid sweatpants. He could almost see the question forming in her head. Why you need two guns? What kinda leather is this? Where's that blunt you rolled?

Why? Why? Why?

If not for her big mouth, Weezy thought she would make for a good piece of arm candy.

His phone rang in his pocket. He pulled it out, saw that it was Lil D, his chief of security, and answered the FaceTime video call.

"What's the word, G."

"Everything's everything," Lil D said. He was light brown in hue and severe in expression with low cut waves and a slightly pudgy face that matched his slightly pudgy body. "We done checked everywhere, and ain't no signs of that old man. I upped the price on his head to a quarter ticket. Hopefully that's get that ball rollin, but it ain't lookin' good. What I know for sure is that he ain't nowhere near Queen of Diamonds. I hired a private security firm to help out, and they got thirty people out here, dressed like regular civilians on the street but they got some real high-tech shit goin' on in these vans and trucks they pulled up in. Buddy in charge of the whole shit gave me a thumbs up 'bout five minutes ago. We're waitin' on you."

Lil D looked a bit more serious than usual, an intensity that Weezy truly appreciated. There was no room for error when it came to old Herbert. Last night's long-range attempt on Millionaire Markio's life had left little doubt as to the old man's deadly aim. Herb was a legitimate threat, a clear and present danger, and Weezy was glad to know that his chief of security pulled out all the stops.

"I'll be on my way out in a minute, G, plenty much," he said.

"Never too much," Lil D replied.

Weezy pocketed his phone and gave into the strong suction of Blicky Nicky's rapidly bobbing mouth. His lower jaw trebled. He took hold of the wide leather armrest and in doing so knocked his towel wrapped bag over ice to the floor. His dick jerked in unison with every warm spurt of semen that was launched into Blicky's persistently sucking mouth, and he could see her throat muscles working overtime to swallow the copious load.

"Ooouuuweee," he said, shuddering. "You the truth. You the world's motherfuckin' greatest."

Blicky Nicky was still pumping his dick in her fist, forcing the last couple of dollops out of him, allowing it to pool in the hollow of his urethral hole before her tongue flicked out to lap it up.

"That was a lot," she said, and cleared her throat. "Tasted good, though. Cum is good for you, you know; for me, I mean." She laughed at the verbal faux pas. "Obviously not for you. But it's full of protein, and it's even good to use as a facial cream. I saw that on Windy Cit—"

"Shut up, Nicky. Just be quiet for one minute."

The girl went quiet, but it was clearly a struggle. She got up and across the floor to one of the closed curtains and peeked out through the crack. Then she started bouncing her ass to some beat only she could hear.

Weezy made a call to Mondo, who told him that his security team was waiting for him in the Sheraton's multi-level parking garage, five vehicles deep and armed to the teeth.

He stopped by the bedroom and found Mikayla lying in bed wit her eyes on the 85-inch flat screen. She was watching *The Real Baddies of Chicago*. The cast of the show was gathered inside the Lincoln Park Zoo's penguin exhibit, fawning over one of the fat little birds while Aqua made a dramatic attempt at feeding the thing.

"I'ma be at the club," Weezy said entering his walk-in closet to put on his shoulder holsters and a black leather Dior jacket. "Text me if you need anything."

"That bitch called me Warm Spice."

Weezy chuckled. "She don't mean no harm."

"I can't stand to hear her fucking voice, and I just met the bitch. She talks way, way, way, way too much. I've never seen anything like her. She has to be high on something."

"Nope. That's just her. Big Gabby put her on Prime Shift just so she could tell her all the gossip."

"Be safe out there, Weezy."

He planted his hands on the soft Gucci comforter and leaned in for a kiss, and Mikayla molded her lips against his. He tasted the grapes she'd just eaten on her tongue. She wore her curly red hair in a natural afro. The five-carat diamond nose-ring in her right nostril had cost Weezy seven thousand dollars.

"Facetime me when you get horny," he said turning to leave. He heard her suck her teeth and smiled. I gotta make it back home to her, he thought to himself and maybe he would.

But then again, maybe he wouldn't.

Chapter 18

"You did a good deed, Little D," Herb said, puffing on his unfiltered Pall Mall and aiming his .45 at the chubby man's chest. "You're a smart man. Lotta guys in your little street gang wouldn't have made that decision. Lotta guys would've died for the cause. Like your friend here, for instance."

Herb canted his head toward the fat little guy's dead friend. A warm corpse that lay stretched in the barren backyard of a tall brick apartment building that stood like a pale red sentry at the corner of 73rd Street and Evans Avenue. There was a wet red hole in the dead man's right eyebrow. The exit wound was a grisly chasm at the back of his head. A sizable portion of his scalp, dread still attached, was still sliding its way down the side of a trash bin in the alleyway fifteen feet behind him. He had died because he had reached for that gun in his belt even after Herbert had warned him against such a move.

Gossamer wisps of smoke wavered lazily in front of the smooth black silencer Herb had screwed into the barrel of his Beretta.

"I ain't no dummy," Lil D said holding his hands in the air while Tiffany pat searched him, stripping him of the Glock in his waistband, his phone, his wallet, a set of keys, and a rubber banded fold of cash, all of which Tiffany stowed away in her YSL shoulder bag.

"Weezy got seventy, eight million dollars. His family's straight if he dies. All I go to my name is a few hundred thousand, and I got seven kids. I'm tryna live for them. Fuck Weezy. You gon' kill that man one way or the other. It ain't no sense in dying with him."

"Oh, how right you are," Herb said, nodding in the affirmative. He peered over Lil D's wide, round shoulder. On the opposite side of the alley was Queen of Diamonds, and where the building ended a chain-link fence began, standing twelve feet high and topped with triple rolls of razor wire, the fence enclosed the entire parking lot.

"So, what now?" Lil D asked.

"Now," Herb said, lowering his pistol, "You take your friend here by the wrist and drag him out to the garbage bin. I want you to stuff him in there. Toss that piece of his scalp in with him. And hurry it up."

Muttering a low string of expletives, Lil D got to work. Tiffany and Herb followed him up the concrete walkway, being careful to step around the drops of blood, and when the dead man's Balenciaga shoe came off, Tiffany squatted to pick it up.

There were six more dead men in the vicinity. Herb had killed them all. He'd seen right through their freshman attempts at counter surveillance, and now they were just warm corpses in their three SUV's, all of which were parked in the far corners of the Queen of Diamonds parking lot.

"I think we should get rid of the girl with all the scary movie tattoos," Tiffany suggested. "She know entirely too much. What if she decides to contact the police?"

"I had thought of that," Herb said, smoking his cigarette and watching as Weezy's corpulent minion lifted the dead man by the armpits and began the arduous task of folding him over into the trash bin. "But she's a co-conspirator, at least she will be a few minutes from now, and I don't see her risking the loss of all that money. She told Karionna about some screenplay she wrote that she's trying to get made into a movie. She'll view that half a million as a kind of necessary evil, if you know what I mean. Like in that old John Wayne flick where Wayne had a team up with one bad guy to take out the other."

Tiffany said, "Nobody watches John Wayne movies anymore."

And at the same time, just as Lil D was shoving his deceased friend's legs into the bin, he said, "*Half a million?*" He wiped some blood on the dead man's pantleg." Sound like I been working for the wrong nigga."

Tiffany tittered behind her black Nike Covid 19 mask, a dark relic from the locked down months of yesteryear. "That was actually Harmonique's money," she said. "I mean, don't get me wrong, we have our own money, and plenty of it, but the money we gave that girl came out of the four million Harmonique gave us to hunt down Baby Stone's killers. She was engaged to Baby Stone, and she watched him get killed right there on the sidewalk outside her designer clothing store."

Lil D frowned. "Weezy ain't' have shit to do with that."

"I know," Herb said, "But that amount he put on my head is really hindering me from being able to focus all my attention on Markio. Now come on into the truck."

The truck was a dark blue Range Rover. It was parked one house down, right up against the QOD parking lot fence. Herb had come close to murdering Lil D as he sat in the driver's seat, but the chubby man had wisely raised his hands in surrender.

Now the three of them climbed into the Rover, Lil D in front, Tiffany and Herb in back.

"Give him his phone," Herb said. "The Weasel might call back. Wouldn't want him suspecting anything."

"Don't shoot me, man." Lil D reached up and turned the rearview mirror until his eyes and Herb's were perfectly aligned. "Don't shoot me in the back of my head or no shit like that."

"I will if you say that again."

"Well, I ain't gon' say that again."

Tiffany snickered. She handed the man his phone. She had put on a fresh pair of black latex gloves, the same brand Herb wore. Her YSL sunglasses had dark lenses, and together with the Covid mask, they made for the perfect disguise.

"Any way I can make me a half million dollars?" Lil D asked.

"Maybe, give me a minute. Need to think." Herb mashed his cigarette in the ashtray, dropped the butt in his pants pocket. And sat back in his seat, gazing out his window and through the chain link at the blue painted rear exit door of Queen of Diamonds. The only vehicle occupying the RESERVED PARKING section was the white Porsche SUV that belonged to the big girl who ran the show when Weezy was away. Herb had seen her inside the club the day he chopped off The Weasel's right hand. It took him twenty seconds to come up with her name. "Gabby," he murmured audibly. "Big Gabby."

Ten seconds later, Tiffany's phone rang with a call from Tylisha. She answered it on speaker.

"They're pulling out of the garage now," Tylisha said, and was that fear in her voice? Herb's brow wrinkled at the sound of it. "He's in the Batur, third car in the motorcade."

Herb's leathery old ace formed a triumphant little grin. His tongue went between his teeth as he prepared to repeat the catchy phrase he'd stolen from *Sanford and Son*—"This is the Big One!" – but he never even got the first syllable out, because Tylisha spoke again, this time in a heart stopping panic.

"Oh my God, I think he spotted me!"

Chapter 19

It wasn't actually Weezy who identified the girl.

"Look," Blicky Nicky said, pointing. "That's one of the old man's girlfriends. She was sitting next to him at that table when he whipped out that sword on you. I swear, it's her. Gabby must've let me see that video a hundred times. She's one of the girls. Same hair, same eyes, same shoulders. Similar pantsuit. Only thing missing is the Covid mask."

Weezy was just nosing the front end of his Bentley coupe up the incline of the parking garage ramp when Blicky pointed the girl out, a dark skinned young woman in a pantsuit with hair that was long on one side and short on the other. The girl was standing on the opposite side of the street, looking right at Weezy's car as it came creeping up over the lip of the ramp, talking to her phone and trying to look as if she wasn't talking about the car she was staring at.

Two Trackhawks led the way, and three more SUVs trailed the Batur as it pulled out onto the street. Weezy braked the car to a stop with his rear tires still on the ramp. His heart pounded. His breathing became shaky. He looked in every direction, throwing himself back in his seat, halfway expecting a bullet to puncture his windshield any second now.

"This hoe got the game fucked up," Blicky Nicky said, and threw open her door. She was out of the car before Weezy could say a word.

"Ay! Ay! Bitch, you hear me! Come 'ere! I wanna show you this uppercut my daddy taught me!"

A Lincoln Town Car came sliding to a halt as Blicky Nicky went sprinting across the street, her eyes locked on the girl in the pantsuit. The girl turned around in a hurry and reached to grab the door handle to the mirrored glass building she'd been loitering in front of, but Blicky Nicky was a fast runner, even in heels. She got close enough to slip her fingers into the girl's hair, balled her hand in a fist with the hair trapped inside it, and shoved the bitch's head face first into the glass door, using all the momentum of her run.

The sheer force of the shove proved to be too much for the pane of glass. It shattered, embedding multiple shards in the flesh of the girl's face. Her nose shattered, too with cartilage snapping like a twig underfoot. A squeak of a shout blew from her bloodied lips as Blicky Nicky yanked her head back and spit in her face

"Aww," Blicky said in her most childlike voice," Your face looks like ground beef. You should really go and get that checked out. I know a great doctor. He's expensive, but I don't think you have much of a—"

The explosion was cataclysmic.

Blicky Nicky's mocking words ceased abruptly. The percussion from the deafening blast blew her clear through the broken glass door. She tumbled and rolled and slid into the building's magnificent lobby, and when she came to a stop she looked up, all disheveled and thunderstruck, thinking that maybe she'd picked the wrong day to cut across the street in front of that Town Car, that maybe the driver was having a bad day and had backed up a few yards and rammed her to hell for making it worse.

But then she looked outside, through wide open spaces that had been towering panes of mirrored glass just two or three seconds ago, and saw the destruction where the Batur had been when she climbed out of it a moment earlier.

Now there was only a huge crater, charred and smoking, in the place where the Batur had sat idling, and the vehicles that had led and trailed it had been knocked aslant. The Town Car was a few yards back, but clearly it had not arrived there on its own volition; it lay inverted on the sidewalk facing the direction from which it had come, crushed beneath its own weight. Bits and pieces of the Bentley rained down from the sky above.

"Okay," Blicky Nicky said admittedly, as a hulking black male security guard came running to her aid, "My daddy ain't prepare me for no shit like this."

Chapter 20

The monotonously incessant *chop-chop-chop* of helicopter rotor blades alerted Princess to her party's arrival.

She was tying the bootstrings of Vee's cute little gray Chanel winter boots when she heard it.

"I believe that's our ride," Prinny said, rising from a squat and zipping up Vee's Chanel bubble jacket in the same motion. "Go down the hall and hug your Auntie Aqua goodbye."

"M'kay"

Prinny shouldered her purse and watched her miniature clone go tearing out of the bathroom… only to come running back in five seconds later, her eyes wide with fear, her braids bouncing wildly about her head. She ran around Princess and cowered low beside the bed, watching the doorway as if she expected a monster to appear at any second.

"Vee," Prinny said, amused. "Who are you hiding from?"

The question was answered a second later, and it came in the form of Davion "Day-Day" Carroll, the 6'7" Dallas Mavericks shooting guard who'd cheated on Aqua with Shmoney Rose before making it right with an enormous diamond engagement ring and a few million dollars in her checking account. His complexion was light brown, like his warmly inviting eyes, and his handsome face was framed by shoulder-length dreadlocks. He wore a brown Nike tee over fitted jeans and size 18 Nike "Day-Day" 4's.

"Why did she just run from me like that?" Day-Day asked.

"You gotta ask her," Prinny said "Because I don't have a clue."

Slowly and watchfully, Vee moved from the relative safety of the bedside to a spot just behind where her mother stood. She peeked around Prinny's hip and stared, saying nothing.

"When did you get in?" Prinny asked.

"Few minutes ago. Aqua's in the shower. I told her a helicopter just landed in her backyard. She said it's definitely for you."

"Yeah, I texted and told her I had somebody coming to pick me up. I didn't think they'd show up in a goddamn helicopter."

"*Two* helicopters," Day-Day corrected, holding up his two fingers for emphasis. "One's still in the air. Is that Queen A?"

Prinny shrugged. "She's who I called, but I'm not sure if she's coming herself or just sending for me."

"That must be pretty cool, having Alexus as a close friend. I met her once, back when she and Bulletface lived in Micheal Jordan's old mansion in Highland Park. They had a pool party, and one of my boys got an invite, let me tag along. I took a pic with a few of the bros, and she was right there in the background. Who'd have thought she'd one day surpass Elon Musk to become the wealthiest person on earth?"

"Money ain't everything." Prinny reached behind her and took hold of Vee's little hand. "Take Aqua, for instance. She's got a fiancé who's a big time NBA player, she's a famous reality TV star, and yet she's flat broke, so broke that she went and did something for a drug kingpin just to hold her over for a while."

Day- Day furrowed his brow. "What? She ain't broke. I just gave her three million last year."

"She burned through that months ago," Prinny said walking toward the door. "Pay more attention to your fiancée. I know you're always on the road, and I respect you putting your career first, but your woman needs you."

"I'ma try and do better."

Princess didn't feel the need to say anything more, so she ambled past him and turned right, holding Vee's hand as the cautious kid trotted forward with her head twisted backward, keeping her untrusting eyes on the man.

"Mommy, he's so, he's so tall," Vee whispered conspiratorially.

"He's definitely tall," Prinny conceded.

"Like the man jack saw at the top of the beanstalk?"

Prinny cracked up laughing. She wished she'd had the foresight to record video of Vee's reaction to the man who must have looked like a veritable giant from her low vantage point.

It took them a couple of minutes to make it to the back of the house. Vee gasped at the sight of the black helicopter that had landed in the east expanse of manicured lawn behind the mansion, but Prinny's gaze locked onto the second chopper that was hovering in the sky above. She could see two men in the open sliding door. One of them was keeping vigil through binoculars, while the other sat behind a long-barreled rifle. Two other men sat in the opposite door, observing the land on that side.

Two brawny Mexican men in black, finely tailored suits climbed out of the grounded chopper and ushered Princess and her daughter inside where Queen A herself sat buckled into one of the black leather seats; she smiled at Vee and made a hand sign to Bojo, the seven-foot Mexican man who sat next to her. He and the other six bodyguards holstered their side arms.

"I didn't know they had this many seats in a helicopter," Prinny remarked as the big black bird took to the sky.

"Bell just recently got this model pushed through the FAA certification process," Alexus said, waving a hand at the interior. "It's the brand new 525 Relentless. Seats sixteen passengers and two pilots can cruise at 184 miles per hour for a range of 667 miles. This baby's got it all"

Alexus Costilla had the most verdant green eyes Princess had ever seen; maybe it was a mental thing, brought on by Prinny's knowledge of the beautiful women's immense wealth, but she didn't think that was the case. Queen A possessed the natural sort of beauty that no man or woman could deny; from her long waterfall of raven black hair and those luxuriant green eyes to her juicy pink lips and voluptuous curves. She was The Real Baddie of America. Clad in a heavy white fur coat that went all the way down to the ankles of her white croc-skin high heeled boots, she looked every bit of as wealthy as the truly was.

"Oh, and it's armored, too," Alexus continued. "There's no chance of that old fuck's Winchester penetrating this bird. Absolutely zero."

Prinny's expression turned quizzical. "Old man."

Alexus nodded. "Herbert Harris. Baby Stone's uncle. He's the House of Lords shooter, so I presume his two young mistresses carried out the Trumbull Avenue bombing."

"And you know this for a fact?"

"I do. Here. See for yourself."

Alexus opened her hand, and Bojo placed an iPhone on her palm. She reached out and gave the phone to Prinny. Five seconds later, Prinny was watching the video.

Shot from a high-tech Panteon camera that must have been concealed somewhere behind one of the brick pillars at the entrance to the house of Lords driveway, the video showed Herb backing into the drive before getting out and popping the trunk of his dark colored Honda. From the trunk he retrieved a tripod, which he took his time assembling, and then a rifle case. The camera was of such high quality that, even in the dark of night, it revealed the suave suited rifleman in great detail leaving no doubt as to the man's identity.

"The man may be old as dirt," Alexus said, "But he's still a highly decorated Vietnam war veteran, justly famed for his skill with a rifle. His military record cites two hundred and nineteen long distance kills, one from nineteen hundred yards. I think he's come to the conclusion that Millionaire Markio ordered Baby Stone's murder, and now he's out for revenge."

"But Markio didn't …He told me that wasn't his work, that it must've been the Hobos, or the Row Row Gangster Disciples."

"And you believed him," Alexus said matter of factly. "You ever heard that "Women Lie, Men Lie" song by Yo Gotti and Wayne? It goes "Women lie, men lie; numbers don't lie. That's a true statement. Markio's cousin Slime did the deed for a million-dollar payday. He's back in Baton Rouge now, his hometown in Louisiana. That million dollars made him a boss in the streets of his city, like Youngboy and Boosie. As a matter of fact, Slime and Youngboy actually grew up together. They're in the same gang."

Stunned to silence, her mouth agape, Princess watched the rest of the video with new understanding. Now it all made sense. Herb had learned of Markio involvement in Baby Stone's murder, which had led to the House of Lords shooting and the Trumbull Avenue bombing.

Prinny looked over at Vee, who'd unbuckled herself from the seatbelt and turned around to kneel on her seat and stare out her window with awestruck eyes. Bojo had placed a pair of noise canceling headphones over her little brown ears, making her oblivious to the conversation between her mother and the richest person alive. For this, Prinny was grateful; Baby Stone and Vee's incarcerated father, Veemo, had been best friends and Prinny had no idea what she'd say if Vee were to reveal at Daddy's next visit that Mommy had been sleeping with his best friend's killer.

"That dirty son of a bitch," Prinny said finally.

"I know right? Old man's got balls of steel. Kinda makes you admire him a little bit, doesn't it."

"I'm not talking about Herb. I meant Markio. I've lost contact with most of my childhood friends for sticking it out with him. Everybody believed he had something to do with Baby Stone getting killed and my dumb ass believed him when he said he didn't do it."

"Love is capable of blinding even the most brilliant minds. Regular people like me and you don't stand a chance."

Shaking her head defeatedly, Prinny reached out with the phone Alexus made no attempt at grabbing it, and she didn't need to. Bojo extended one freakishly long arm and effectively plucked the phone from Prinny's fingers.

"I didn't even know there was a camera right there," Prinny muttered vacantly.

"Neither did Markio. In fact, he still don't know. Only reason he knew it was Herb was because Weezy called and told him that Herb had just mentioned an imminent attack against Markio's operation before he came for Weezy later on. Which just happened by the way. Not even five minutes ago. It's breaking news on all the news stations as we speak."

"He killed Weezy?" Prinny asked.

"I don't know yet. They haven't reported any fatalities, but like I said, it just happened. Huge explosion down in Streeterville, right in front of the Sheraton. That's where Weezy lives."

Princess could think of nothing to say, so she said nothing.

"I sent a couple of my guys to have a word with the Hobos, but they were already eliminated from the equation," Alexus went on. "Fed did a sweep this morning, locked up all but one of them, and he's on the run. Guy named Jonesy. He's one of the boys your ex-shot up really bad; Left him in a wheelchair, so I guess he's more on the roll than on the run." Alexus laughed while Prinny showed only the tiniest hint of a smirk. Queen A's laugh was just as soft and pleasing as her voice. "Anyway, the Feds won't be finding him alive, because we found him first."

Prinny sat up straight. She stared at Alexus, searching those sexy green eyes for any telltale signs of humor, and found none. Alexus rotated her wrist and opened her hand. Bojo set the iPhone on her palm and she offered it to Princess.

"Take a look."

She told Prinny where to find the video, in a text message thread, not the gallery where the other video was stored, and Prinny pressed the triangular Play icon.

It was a short video, just seven seconds in length, and it began as an SUV full of Spanish speaking men pulled up alongside a dusty black GMC pickup truck. Jonesy sat in the passenger seat with his arm out the window, patting his finger on the roof and bobbing his head to the beat of an old Bump J track he had blaring from the sound system. The driver of the pickup was a young black man with a round face and a shiny bald head. Prinny recognized him as DJ, a former Gutterville Mickey Cobra turned Hobo. Jonesy didn't even look at the Hispanic men but DJ did. His eyes got big as the Hispanic driver and the man seated behind him struck their arms out the windows with Glocks in their hands. They opened fire. Round after round rocked Jonesy's head, which went from a honey brown homely thing to a bloody mess within a couple of seconds. DJ pushed open his door and was diving out of harm's way when two or three rounds hit the back of his head. He went stiff and dropped out of sight, and the video ended.

Prinny looked up from the phone without lifting her head. Only her eyes rose. Alexus was looking right at her, and now there was no doubt about it: all traces of humor had vanished from those pretty green eyes. Replacing it, was cold, bottomless evil, not directed at Prinny, but at the situation in general. A protective evil.

"My men are searching for Herb now," Alexus said. "We just received the GPS coordinates to his cell phone. He was right behind Queen of Diamonds a few minutes ago, but he's on the move now, heading west. He'll be dead before—"

The phone in Prinny's had begun to ring just then.

"Bojo," said the queen. "Answer that."

Bojo took the phone from Prinny and answered the call. He spoke a few words in Spanish.

"Seven dead bodies," Alexus said, returning her ice-cold gaze to Prinny's baffled one. "Won't be any pussy popping tonight."

"What happened?" Prinny asked.

"Old Herbert's struck again. The police were called to investigate a SUV in the parking lot at Queen of Diamonds. Two unresponsive subjects were seated in the driver and passenger seats, bleeding profusely from the head. When the police arrived, they found two more SUV's parked in the other corners of the parking lot, each one with two more dead bodies sitting inside. And there was a seventh body stuffed in a trash can in the alley behind the club. It's the old man for sure. Nobody heard or reported any gunshots so he used a silencer. He's like Denzel in the Equalizer, only there's no director to yell "Cut!" This is the real deal. I wonder what made him snap, and on today of all days."

"Weezy," Princess said. "Weezy came back in town last night. He must've been waiting on that moment."

"But how did he find out where Markio's stash house was located? The House of Lords, that address is public information, but I want to know how he found the stash house." Alexus paused, thinking. The massive diamond on her ring finger twinkled in the sunlight.

Prinny was also thinking: about the time Alexus had been arrested for firing a handgun at her rap star Hubby's tour bus while he was inside it; about the time Alexus was indicted for a slew of charges that included multiple murders, kidnapping, briberies, extortions, and an allegation that she and the arrest of the Costilla clan had smuggled thousands of kilograms of narcotics into the United States of America; about the often repeated rumor that all of Mexico's drug cartels had come together under one umbrella, and the head of that umbrella was the Matamoros cartel, that the Matamoros cartel was really the Costilla Cartel, and the top boss of the Costilla Cartel was the quarter trillion dollar women herself, Mrs. Alexus Costilla-King.

Roughly half of America believed wholeheartedly in the rumors, while the other half believed there was no way an American born woman of such great beauty and high intellect would ever even consider getting involved with a Mexican drug cartel, whether she was half Mexican or not.

Princess had considered herself part of the latter group.

Now, though-now, she wasn't so sure.

"Well, however he found out," Alexus said, apparently having given up trying to figure it out herself, "He's gonna regret ever doing it. And that's on my father's gravestone."

Chapter 21

Just below the Costilla Hotel and Towers' rooftop lounge sat the single most expensive apartment in downtown Chicago. Spanning three floors and sprawled across seventeen thousand square feet of living space, with white marble floors and gray marble walls, the condominium was worth a reported $95 million.

Blake King rarely set foot in most of the rooms. The thirty-three-year-old rap god, known all around the world as Bulletface, spent more time in his state of the art recording studio than he did anywhere else.

He was inside the soundproof booth, listening to a drill beat he'd purchased from Young Chop through his gilded headphones, smoking a morbidly fat blunt of Raspberry Gelato and sipping from a tall Styrofoam cup of Lean while he thought over the lyrics he'd freestyle over the track. Through the glass and beyond the soundboard where his music engineer sat waiting on him to go in, the door that opened into the hallway swung inward and Millionaire Markio strode in followed by one of the thickest, most beautiful chocolate-hued women Blake had ever seen. He knew the girl. She was Kamari White, Princess Kelly's half-sister. Blake thought she looked like Chiney Ogwumike.

Young Meach—Money Bagz Management's most successful recording artist next to Bulletface – came in behind Kamari, ogling her fat ass out the corner of his eye. Deja and Young Nya, female rap artists who had both gone platinum since signing with MBM, were the last to come through the door. Deja reached back and pushed the door shut behind her.

Looking out at his iced out coterie of rap stars, Bulletface found easy inspiration. Young Nya was a street legend in the city of Chicago. Before being signed, she and her husband— Kamari's deceased father, Lejon "Grizzy" White—had gone to war with several different gangs on the city's west side, and though Nya had never been arrested, everyone knew that she had personally committed at least half a dozen murders on her own, especially after Grizzy was gunned down, while they were enroute to what would have been her first paid show. She was the raw epitome of a bad bitch, short and light skinned and pretty as can be. Her hair was jet black. The double G pendant hanging from her icy Cuban-link neck was identical to the Gucci symbol, only hers stood for Grizzy Gang. Like the other rappers she wore glistening white diamonds around her neck, wrist and fingers, and high end designer gear from head to toe.

Like Young Nya, Deja had assimilated to Hip Hop's recent shift toward the stripper hoe culture. Her brown leather pants looked painted on. She was a short, pretty girl like Nya, just two or three shades browner and an inch or so taller. Her longtime boyfriend D Boy was also signed to MBM. She possessed an uniquely beautiful smile— unlike Nya, who hardly smiled at all— and the kind of disposition that made her fans admire her even more.

The only one Bulletface truly believed could compete with him bar for bar was Demetrius Burns, Aka Young Meach, aka YM. Maybe that opinion was biased, seeing as they had been friends since their childhood in Michigan City, Indiana. Meach's rap game had come a long way since then; he had four Grammys to show for it, as well as a number of gold and platinum plaques he'd accumulated over the years. He wore a Dior bandana draped over his head, a Dior sweatshirt, Amiri jeans and Dior sneakers. A Glock

23 pistol was wedged behind his Dior belt. He stopped in the middle of the room, folded his muscular arms across his equally muscled chest and canted his head to the side, daring Bulletface to go hard.

And then there was Millionaire Markio.

Short and strongly built, loyal to his friends and sheer hell on his enemies, Markio was one of the only men Bulletface knew with a reputation for gun violence that rivaled his own. He was a Chicago gang star who'd wreaked havoc on Michigan City in the early 2000's before Blake became Bulletface. How he'd gone on to become a best-selling novelist with a movie that had debuted at the #1 spot at the box office was not unlike the way Blake had gone from a drug dealing gunslinger to an acclaimed gangsta rapper and the CEO of one of the hottest record labels in the music industry. Markio was dapper in a Louis Vuitton jogger that was black like his skullcap, sneakers, and backpack, all of which were fashioned by the same designer.

The microphone suspended from the ceiling above BulletFace was coated with gold like his headphones. He motioned for his music engineer –Johnathan "J-Bo" Compton, a lanky 23-year-old with cornrows and big ears to restart the beat, and then he toked on his blunt, stepped up to the mic, and started in.

"It's Bulletface, you know I'll fuck 'round a pull a K. We hop out, walk 'em down how we demonstrate
And we GDK, say at shit til I'm blamed away
What's my plan today? Murder you and yo' fam today
So good night, boa, like Markio I'm a Vice Lord
Try and take my life, we gon' fight fo' it
Got YM wit' me, he hype fo' it
Glizzy on him right now, nigga, I'm lookin at it as I speak
Lord there wit that Draco in his backpack, he a beast…"

Millionaire Markio's mouth parted in awe. How does he *do* that shit? Was the thought that ran through his mind as he and Kamari seated themselves in two of the eight swivel chairs that were scattered haphazardly across the red carpeted floor. He's been invited into the studio three times before, and each time he's been just as awestruck by Blake's ability to make rhymes out of things he saw in front of him, or the things that were going on in the music industry and in this personal life – all without ever writing a single word of it down.

"That nigga is raw," Markio said, enunciating each word for emphasis. "He saw me swinging this backpack off my shoulder, saw the butt of my Draco sticking out of it, and came up with that. "Draco in his backpack' line on the spot."

"I grew up on Bulletface," Kamari said, "Had his poster on the wall right next to my bed. My mama said he's to my generation what 50 Cent was to hers, a gangsta nigga who's been shot a buncha times."

Markio gave her no reply. He sipped from his double stacked cup of Wockhardt and Sprite and continued listening to Bulletface's grimy flow. It was difficult to focus with all the beauty surrounding him. A black woman with a fat ass was his kryptonite, his Achilles heel, and there were three of them in the room with him.

Kamari's phone lay on her thigh. It buzzed once and she ignored it. Five seconds or so later, it buzzed again. And this time she checked it.

"Oh, my fuckin God," she said. "Markio, I'm about to send you this link. You gotta see this."

Markio waited for his phone to vibrate in his pocket before he took it out to view the link she'd sent him. He saw what it was and immediately shook his head in disbelief. It was a *TMZ News* link. The headline read "Princess Kelly suffers MELTDOWN After Catching Millionaire Markio in bed with her SISTER!" And there was video, captured from inside the House of Lord garage, showing her screaming about the incident while her daughter tried to sleep on her shoulder—and also while a craps game took place just eight or nine feet behind her. Markio appeared late in the video after Princess had disappeared into the backset of Bam's Cullinan outside the garage, but she climbed right back out of the Rolls Royce to scream curses at him directly before getting in and ordering Bam to drive away.

This day just keep getting worse, Markio thought to himself, because watching the video made him think of the man who'd been shot and killed in the very same garage roughly ninety minutes later. And of the $15.3 million in cash he'd lost in the Trumbull Avenue bombing. He was heated – *overheated* really – about the whole situation, but what could he do? He was accustomed to driving down on his opposition and jumping out on them with his gun in hand. How was he going to find a 81 year old man? He'd called Aunt Bone and asked her if she'd seen her husband.

"He bet not show his face in my house! Bastard lied to me, talking about them two strumpets was his assistant and his driver. I look like I got fool written across my damn head?" Markio had chuckled once, a chuckle so dry it died of thirst, and he'd ended the call with no more information than he'd had at the start of it.

He sipped his Lean, realizing he was self-medicating and not really giving a fuck about it. He'd lost $15.3 million. He deserved to get high.

However upset he might be, he couldn't deny that there was a silver lining to it all. Tayja and her sons had, Thank God, gone down the block to a birthday party Rev the barber had invited her to shortly before the bombing took place. The only casualty was Back Down, Rev's three year old pit bull terrier. Not to discredit Rev's love for his canine companion, for he had already posted a tearful video to Facebook, saying his goodbyes to Back Down and regaling his five thousand "friends" with tales of the many adventures he'd had with the loyal young pit.

And there was another silver lining one that took precedence over all others: he was alive. The bullet that debrained Lil Archie had been meant for him, and the man he'd called Uncle Herb for most of his life had fired the shot.

It was crazy how people changed.

"Where's Alexus?" Kamari asked in a whisper. "I thought she said she'd be here."

"She'll be here," Markio whispered back. "I think she was going to check on Princess."

"Hope she don't bring her over here. I ain't tryna beat her ass, but I will if I have to."

Markio thought that fight might go the other way, but he didn't say it. He slurped some Lean and listened to Bulletface. Kamari silenced her ringer as the calls about the TMZ video started pouring in. Soon Markio's phone was buzzing and ringing too. He checked the notifications without any particular feelings toward the text messages and Instagram comments. He saw that the video was also on The Shade Room, and a dozen other gossip pages. His cousins Candace, Tweety, Ernie, Chanel, and Bear all texted him within seconds of each other, each with a different link to a video of Prinny's so called meltdown. He tried to remember who he'd seen holding up a phone in the garage and couldn't so he went to his Panteon home security app, rewound the saved footage and watched it again—for the umpteenth time today.

He knew exactly where to look, so he found it in seconds. Gucci Ball was the culprit. He'd gone from filming a few of the girls twerking to recording the video of Prinny's meltdown.

"That bitch-ass nigga," Markio mumbled.

"Is that Gucci Ball?" Kamari asked, leaning toward him. "I know that ain't Gucci Ball."

"That's definitely him"

"Why would he do some bullshit like that?"

"Fuck if I know." Gucci Ball was gang, one of the TVL's who's been with the mob since way back when. His cousin was none other than Trav of the Sicko Mobb rap duo, but he was famed for selling high end designer gear at low end prices. "I know he got me fucked all the way up, though. On Cup grave. Wait till I see—"

Right then, as if Gucci Ball or Rodrick Case, as his mother had named him, had secretly bugged Markio's phone and heard his name being spoken against, Markio's phone rang with a call from the man himself.

"Joe, on Cup I ain't do that shit," he said urgently "My lil bitch just woke me up an showed me this Shade Room post. I know it's the video I recorded, but I ain't sent that to nobody. I ain't even posted it on the Gram. Apple must've hacked into my shit—the company I mean, not our homie?"

"How the fuck it get online if you didn't post it, Lord? Somebody had to send that shit out."

"Gang, on fo'nem grave ain't nobody … wait I did let one lil thotty use my shit to put her number in my phone. Bad lil Puerto Rican bitch who couldn't stop talkin'. Damn, and I had just showed her that video. Wait a minute, I got her name in my phone.

There was a brief pause. Some fumbling on Gucci Ball's end, a young woman's voice could be heard saying, "I ain't no lil bitch, either."

Gucci Ball replied. "What, you want me to say my big bitch? I try to show you some love and this the thanks I get? Boy, you hoes ain't shit."

Markio was on his Panteon home security app as Gucci Ball and his lil bitch bickered back and forth, He found the segment of video showing Gucci Ball handing his phone to the bad lil Puerto Rican bitch and immediately knew who she was. It was Blicky Nicky, the girl all the QOD dancers called Blabbermouth Blicky, the girl Cherish Taylor and Shmoney Rose had practically *begged* Princess not to add to the cast of their reality show.

"The girl talks entirely too much," Cherish had explained.

Shmoney had seconded the motion." I'm telling you Prinny, that bitch would make my fuckin *head* explode."

Markio had heard the conversation because it had been broadcast from the speakers in Prinny's Maybach. They had been on their way home from the Brickyard Mall when she took the call, and he remembered her hanging up and saying she should put the girl on the show anyway, just to spite bitches.

"Here it go right here," Gucci said. "Blicky Nicky. Man, that bitch is bad. Nigga. Ass so fat need a lap dance. She must've sent the video to her phone when I let her put her number in here."

"Yeah, I know. I'm lookin' at the garage video."

"Sneaky bitch. She got down on me, Lord. You know I wouldn't do you like that."

"You know she saved Ton's life last night?"

"Man, that bitch can save my life any day. On fo'nem. I was thinkin about slidin' up there to Queen of Diamonds tonight, but you see dat shit on the news?"

"See what on the news?" Markio asked.

"Nigga, on Cup, they just found seven dead bodies in the QOD parkin' lot. Two mo' in the alley. They say whoever did it must've used a sound suppressor, 'cause ain''t nobody hear the shots. A sound suppressor, that's like a silencer. Ain't it?"

"Yeah, Ay, I'ma hitchoo back. And stop recordin' shit ol 'police ass nigga."

"My bad, Lord. On gang, that's my bad, Lord."

Markio ended the call and searched Chicago News on Google. The first thing that popped up was another bombing and this time it was a car bombing in front of the Sheraton Suites in the affluent Streeterville neighborhood, of all places.

The second link was the same story, but the third one down, a Fox32 news link, was the one Markio was looking for. Gucci Ball had exaggerated the body count, but he was close enough. Six men had just been found dead inside their vehicles in the Queen of Diamonds parking lot from apparent gunshot wounds, and a seventh body had been discovered inside a trash bin in the alleyway behind the gentlemen's club.

That was all Uncle Herb, Markio thought, because he knew it. He knew it like he knew his own name, like he knew the Department of Corrections number he'd been identified by for fifteen years. Uncle Herb was at it again, and this time he wasn't fucking around.

Rev, Markio's barber and the owner of the Trumbull Avenue home that had been blown to smithereens, called Markio's phone just as Bulletface exited the thick glass door of his recording booth—to an exultant round of applause from his fellow rap stars—and motioned for Markio and Kamari to follow him out into the hallway. Markio shouldered the backpack and answered the call as he went.

"Yoooo," Markio said, "What's the word, Big Breed?"

Rev was a member of the Black Ganster New Breeds, a gang that on the west side of Chicago had too many members to enumerate.

"Man, these alphabet boys just showed up outside my girl's crib talm 'bout they want me to come with them. My girl answered the door. I just heard the shit from the bedroom. You know why they want me, right?"

Of course, Markio knew why the feds wanted to speak with Rev. They wanted to know where all the blown up cash had come from. But Markio wasn't going to discuss it over the phone.

"Man, I don't know shit," he said "And you don't know shit. Lawyer up on 'em as soon as you get in there. Tell 'em our lawyer is Nikkia Staples, and when you call just say I hired her for you a month ago. She'll come and get you out. Aight?"

"You just make sure to call that woman now, so she'll know to be expecting my call."

'I'm on it, bruh."

The three of them were standing in the marble floored hallway when Markio pocketed his steadily ringing phone – Markio, Kamari and Bulletface.

There were two visible scars on the left side of Blake's face. Circular in shape and shade darker than his regular dark hued skin tone. They were bullet wounds from thirteen or fourteen years prior, healed over now but still clearly distinguishable. He was tall, dark and remarkable handsome – the sort of man all the women drooled over – so it was no real surprise that he'd become such a sex symbol over the span of his career.

But make no mistake about it, through and through, Bulletface was a gangster. The gold-plated Desert Eagle .50 caliber pistol he had holstered under his left arm wasn't there for show. The many other bullet scars that pocked his skin all over weren't from his being strung up and used as someone's target at a gun range. It was rumored that before his stellar rap career, he'd gone from dealing grams and ounces of crack-cocaine to moving hundreds of kilos and he'd suffered all the inexorably dangerous pitfalls that come with the lifestyle—broad daylight shootouts, robbery attempts gang wars and rap beefs and a hundred other drug related obstacles and he'd come out of it with a sterling reputation an eight billion dollar new worth.

It also didn't hurt that his wife was worth $250 *billion*.

The man wore a black and red Versace tee, a red Versace belt with a gold buckle black fitted jeans with red fabric peeking out from beyond the ragged tears across the legs, and a black and red pair of Jordan 5s. Like Markio, he wore a bevy of glittering diamond chains around his neck, and his hair was a fresh fade of low cut waves. The foremost twenty teeth in his mouth were encased in flawless white diamond, and half of them showed in his signature half grin as he looked from Markio to Kamari and back to Markio again.

"Man, y'all both tweakin," he said and sucked smoke from his blunt. "Why would y'all try to do that shit? Y'all know Prinny ain't no dumb bitch. If she was, Alexus wouldn't have brought her on as a producer of that show."

"I ain't even gonna lie, Lord. She sat on my lap and I couldn't even help myself," Markio said, and that was the God's honest truth. Even now, as Kamari stood beside him in her sheer blue Ferragamo bodysuit and off-white Celine Homme sneakers, braless and pantiless so that her boobs and nether lips protruded notably from the fabric, he found it nearly impossible to keep his eyes on the man in front of him.

"Can't say that I blame you for that." Bulletface shot an appraising glance Kamari's way, and the smile she put on said she'd strip naked in a flash if he gave the word. "But she's still your girl's sister. I done did a lotta bullshit, fucked all kinds of hoes, but I ain't never fucked nobody my—"

He froze as he raked his eyes down Kamari's voluptuous curves a second time and when he spoke again it was in a tone of pure resignation. "You know what? I feel you bruh. Alexus didn't have no sisters or cousins thick as she is. Goddamn."

Kamari simpered. "Thank you, Bulletface," she said which was somewhat of a non sequitur as Bulletface had not given her a direct compliment. Standing before her was the same musclebound gangsta rapper she'd probably fantasized about growing up. She was starstruck.

"Was it worth it?" Bulletface asked her.

She nodded. "Best dick I've ever had. Superdick. This man should've been a porn star. I bet you're like that too, huh? We should have a threesome. Or a train. Whatever you call it?"

"If the queen found out, you'd lose either your whole head or the brains inside it. And I'm dead serious."

Kamari's lower lip slid out in a veritable pout. Bulletface sipped his Narco drink and puffed his high grade blunt. Markio silenced a call from his son's mother, Mya Patterson.

And Alexus Costilla came walking up the hallway with her close friend Princess Kelly.

Chapter 22

"Look at this," Tiffany said, pointing her TV remote at her wall mounted flat screen, which was ninety inches wide and took up most of the west wall in the living room of her Gold Coast townhouse.

Herb squinted at the television, though the image on its screen was large and crystal clear. It showed him and Tiffany standing side by side in the alleyway that ran between Evans and Cottage Grove, the two of them seeming to be holding Lil D at gunpoint. She flipped from Fox 32 to MTN 12 from MTN 12 to NBC 5, from NBC 5 to ABC 7 and saw the same image on every channel. It was breaking news. The FBI was offering $50,000 for any information that led to an arrest. The suspects were considered armed and dangerous.

"Damn right we're armed and dangerous," Herb said in his cracked and raspy voice. "More dangerous than you sons of bitches will ever know."

"It's a good thing you wore that hat, and I wore that mask and those sunglasses."

"Certainly is. Certainly is."

The two of them had changed clothes shortly after arriving at Tiffany's million dollar pied a terre. He was cool, calm, and collected in black slacks, a beige and green blazer and black oxfords. Tiffany wore only a black lace Fenty XSavage bra. Her bare bottom was planted on soft brown English leather. Her left hand was closed in a fist, and trapped inside it was Herb's hard, wet penis.

She leaned in over his lap and dropped a fat glob of saliva onto his cockhead. It was the third time she'd done it in the last five minutes.

"Tylisha still hasn't called," she said, tearing up. "That's so not like her. I don't think she made it out of the blast zone."

"She may not have. They're reporting six fatalities and eight more were injured. Critically injured, Ty could be on either side of that equation. It's a possibility that we've gotta prepare ourselves for. Crying about it won't solve a thing. You need to get it out of your head. Focus on something else. Like pleasing me, for instance."

Herb's suggestion elicited a nasal chuckle from Tiffany. She rolled her eyes, smilingly thumbed away her tears, lifted her knees onto the sofa, and lowered her mouth to the erection she'd been stroking ever since Herb came in from their shared bedroom, where he'd spent an hour with Kolita Saint Pierre, the CPD officer of Haitian descent whose unrelenting attempts at joining his cabal of mistresses had finally won him over.

Kolita's vaginal juices still ringed Herb's mouth, sugary orgasmic juices that Tiffany tasted on his dick as she pushed it past the back of her throat.

"Yeah," Herb crooned, sinking his fingers into the soft flesh of her left buttock. "That's it, baby girl. You just focus on this dick in ya mouth. That should take away all the tears."

Tiffany's ability to deepthroat was unrivaled. Herb liked the wet sounds his dick made in her throat. The gagging sounds. He tilted his head back and stared up at the ceiling relishing the memory of bedding Kolita – and not even thinking of Tylisha.

The Haitian woman was twenty four, short and thick with a complexion like coffee with half a teaspoon of milk stirred in it. Herb had always liked thicker women. They were called brick houses, back in his day. The perfume Kolita wore could've made his dick harden without the Viagra tablet he'd taken. He'd ordered her to kneel on the edge of the bed, naked from the waist down and wearing the shirt and cap that went with her police unform. A true cunnilingus connoisseur, Herb had licked and sucked on her pussy for a good long while, twenty or twenty five minutes at least and she'd climaxed three times within that span. Two little orgasms and a hug gusher that had flooded Herb's mouth and dripped from the silver hairs on his chin.

His lower back still ached from the exertion of what had followed. He had guided his hard member into the snug warmth of her dripping hole and fucked her as roughly as he could, partly because he'd never liked cops. Cops had taken his good friend Jeff Fort and locked him away in the Colorado Mountains and also because rough sex was what all young freaks were after these days. The highly romanticized days of Patti Labelle, Diana Ross, and Aretha Franklin were long gone. All that sweet make love to me music had been replaced by prurient, fuck the shit out of me tunes of Cardi B and Sexyy Red. Which Herb enjoyed thoroughly, for to a man his age, there was nothing sweeter than a tight bodied young woman who was willing to submit to his every sexual desire. He'd gone in balls deep and shot his sticky cum load far into the depths of her pussy and he hadn't pulled out until he was certain that every last drop of semen had oozed out of him.

Herb was paying Kolita Saint Piere $25,000 a month for her service and he was determined to get his money's worth.

Looking up at the white stucco ceiling, listening to the wet, squishy noises in Tiffany's throat and the shower water running in the hallway bathroom, Herb thought of The Weasel and smiled. He'd smiled more today than he had in months.

"Pops goes the motherfucking Weasel," Herb whispered victoriously.

He wondered how many ragged, bloody pieces of the man's flesh and bone would be found. Not very many, he decided. The Big One had done old Weasel in. One full pound of C4 explosive, stuck to the Bentley Batur's undercarriage with a prepaid cell phone attached as the detonator, was all it had taken to send Weezy to his maker. And this time there was no mistaken identity. Herb had gotten his man. A few minutes after the man called Lil D had dropped Herb and Tiffany off at Herb's Mulsanne. Tiffany had shown Herb an Instagram video that the girl Kitty Jae called Blabbermouth Blicky had shared with her seven hundred thousand followers

"Oh my God, y'all," Blabbermouth's video commentary began. Her face had been covered in dusty gray ash, a trickle of blood coming out of one nostril and down over her lips and chin, making her resemble those stunned survivors of 9/11 you always caught a glimpse of while thumbing through your TV channels in early September. "These niggas done blew up Weezy. Two million dollars he paid for that spit sneeze car, and he just died in it. Look this his pinkie ring right here, with his pinkie still in the motherfucker."

She'd aimed her high definition smartphone camera right at the severed finger, and Herbert T Harris had rejoiced!

One down. One to go.

It was the thought he'd had then, and the thought he had now.

He lowered his head to look at the television, just as his military profile photo appeared on the screen.

"This just in. Police have now identified 81-year-old Herbert Theodore Harris as the man they believe is responsible for the Queen of Diamonds murders, The House of Lords shooting and both of today's bombings..."

Tiffany popped up like a meerkat who'd heard a suspicious sound. Eyes wide, spit hanging from her chin. She stared at her massive flatscreen, flabbergasted by the news she was hearing.

"…. That federal authorities have taken a female accomplice of Harris' in custody, and she is cooperating with investigators."

Tiffany gasped. "Tylisha!"

"It appears that way," Herb said calmly

"I swear to you, Herb. I have never heard of Tylisha snitching on anybody." She sat up and wiped her face in haste. "That motherfucker Markio. We can't let him live. We can't let him live! I told you what he did to my nieces and nephews. They're scarred for life!"

Tiffany had indeed informed Herb of that particular incident. Apparently, Markio had gunned down some chump in her older sister's living room, right in front of the big sister, their two brothers, and all of their children. The shooting had traumatized the little shittlins. A few of them could no longer stand to watch cartoons. One blast from Yosemite Sam's pistol and they went running for Mommy.

"Get a hold of yourself," Herb said. "Close up those curtains. Go and put some clothes on and bring a towel to dry my roly poly. Can't put it away all wet, now can—"

The front door burst open, and half a dozen men rushed in, moving in military formation, brandishing AR-15s with red beams and sound suppressors, clad in all black with ski masks concealing their faces and bulletproof vests shielding their burly torsos.

Herb's Beretta was holstered under his arm, but he knew better than to make any sudden moves. Tiffany was not as wise. There was a gray steel Remington 870 Brushmaster shotgun lying on the coffee table and she reached for it. A muted rattle of gunfire was sent her way. The rifle slugs nearly sawed her in half, and she was blown halfway across the room. Just as she hit the floor, Herb realized that the armed intruders had yet to identify themselves as police or federal agents.

Slowly, he lifted his hands above his head. The man who'd killed Tiffany moved in and relieved him of his weapon, while two others broke away to search the rest of the town house. Those two returned with Kolita. Still naked from the shower, all of her was relatively dry except for her left leg, which she must have been preparing to dry when they accosted her.

For a moment, no one said a word. Then a tall man in a spiffy white Armani suit and tie, Herb knew his suits, entered through the breached door, and the first thing Herb noted was the man's prosthetic left hand; he'd have been hard pressed not to note it, because the hand was gold. The man had an athletic build, and the black ski mask on his head looked oddly out of place above his rich white threads.

"Stand up," White Suit ordered, so Herb stood up. His pants fell down around his ankles as he rose from the sofa. "Hands behind your back," White suit ordered, so Herb followed that instructions well, turning his back toward the guy who'd just taken a pair of black steel handcuffs from his utility belt.

Herb's dick remained hard all the while, sticking out in front of him with a gleaming sheen of saliva coating it from end to end. White Suit had his men double lock the cuffs once they were in place, and then he had Kolita stow Herb's erection in his boxer shorts and fix his pants around his waist.

Herb said, "Spare the girl, She's innocent."

"Of course I'll spare the girl. She's done nothing wrong," White Suit said, as someone placed a black pillowcase over Herb's head. "It's you the queen wants."

Chapter 23

"You, I understand. You're a man, and men generally aren't shit. But you! You're my sister! How could you betray me like this?"

"I betrayed you? You stole the fucking love of my life! And what about Jabar? What about Jabar!"

Millionaire Markio stood off to the side while the two sisters stood toe-to-toe. They were in a personal hair salon that was more spacious than a lot of salons Markio had taken his girlfriends to over the years . The sink basins were white marble like the flooring. The east wall was one big glass window overlooking Lake Michigan. Oversized smart TVs graced the walls, all of them tuned to an old Jennifer Hudson music video, which was muted for some odd reason. Why anyone would ever silence such a beautiful voice was beyond Markio's realm of understanding. There were five sumptuous white leather chairs for the hairdressing, five more for the hair washing and a row of chairs Markio presumed was for guests.

Eschewing the sibling rivalry, Markio turned and slipped back out into the hallway, where Alexus and her giant bodyguard stood waiting. Alexus squinted at Markio inside the salon; Kamari and Prinny were still exercising their vocal cords.

"First Nikkia," Alexus said bitterly. "Now Princess. You're really pushing it."

Markio licked his lips sucked some air between his two top teeth and sipped some Lean.

"We found Herb," Alexus continued "He's not dead, but soon he will be. You can go on back to the House of Lords and finish up that screenplay. People are waiting for that movie release. Hell, I'm waiting for the movie release."

Markio nodded his head and said nothing. This time his silence appeared to anger Queen A. There was a barely discernible rise to the corner of her mouth, and hot orange flames licked behind the green of her eyes.

"I hope you know that you still owe me twenty-two million dollars," she said snappishly. " I could give two fucks about that house being blown to bits. I want my money Markio, and I want it fast. Do you understand me? "

"Yes, ma'am," Markio said, because that's what you said to people who fronted you 2,000 kilograms of cocaine for $22 million.

"And another thing." She continued. "No more dating my friends from here on out. You are never to date any of my associates. Not Princess, not Nikkia, not anybody. Hire a moving company to pack up Prinny's things, and have them delivered to her place in Highland Park. Break it off with her permanently. You got that?"

"I got it."

"Good. Because we're making too much money to be going through this petty bullshit. Oh, and by the way, the Hobos just got indicted, so that situation is finished. Get back to writing that screenplay and get that money to me yesterday."

Alexus turned tail and stormed away. Markio sipped his drink, watching her go. She wore a snow-white skintight dress and high heeled shoes of the same color . Her ass was just about as fat and round as Kamari's, looking at it made Markio's mouth water.

He shook his head and went walking the other way. Ten minutes later, he was slicing down Lake Shore Drive in his sleek white Lamborghini Aventador, listening to Lil Durk's "Threats to Everybody" with his Draco pistol resting beneath his thigh and considering the unknown threats that lay ahead.

Epilogue:

New Benz, New Friends

Martisha Miller's eyes were a vapid shade of hazel, and she had three cavities in her mouth- two in the teeth on the lower right side of her mouth, and one on the lower left. These facts were apparent to Aqua as soon as she and Day-Day entered Martisha's hospital room, because the girl's eyes and mouth went agape with shock, and she kept that same expression on her pale, gaunt face as the rest of the women from her favorite reality TV show spilled into the room, each of them carrying teddy bears and balloons with lively exhortations imprinted on them.

"Surprise!" Aqua shrieked, a bit on the loud side but what the hell. This was an exciting moment; it deserved some kind of shout.

Martell "Tails" Miller applauded the new arrivals from his big sister's bedside, his chipped teeth on full display. Mrs. Miller was also in attendance, a skinny, attractive women with a great big smile that matched her son's, minus the broken teeth.

The height of the momentous occasion came when Day-Day announced he and Aqua, though Prinny knew it was more like he, alone, would be paying off all of Martisha's hospital bills. That was when her levees broke open. Tears all around and Mike the cameraman caught it all on film from his position in the open doorway.

Making the hospital visit the last segment in the two-hour season finale had been Aqua's idea. After the immense heartache of going to Weezy's funeral two days ago, a portion of which had been filmed and would air in the finale's first hour, the girls needed to end the season on a high note, and what better way to do that than to lift the spirits of a woman who needed it most?

Tearful hugs were given, smiling group photos were taken, and Martisha gained seven more Instagram followers before the visit came to an end. Princess slipped Mrs. Miller a $100,000 check on her way out the door, and the slender woman screamed for Jesus as she wrapped her bony arms around Princess and squeezed stomping the floor with both feet and crying as if she needed to use the bathroom really bad but all were occupied

"You have the biggest heart," Aqua said as the eight of them were marching toward the elevators. She held Prinny's hand in hers and interlaced their fingers together. "I am so proud to call you my best friend."

"I thought I was your best friend," Thick Doll said taking Aqua's other hand.

"You're a different kind of friend." Aqua flickered her long, pierced tongue in Thick Doll's direction, and all the girls laughed—but Princess believed the flirtatious gesture was more real than the other girls realized. It was just over a week ago when she'd gone to Aqua's place after catching Markio and Kamari together, and she clearly remembered seeing that Thick Doll had fallen asleep naked in Aqua's bed.

She'd have to remind herself to do a little digging into that mystery next season.

Day Day and his even taller teammate, Isaiah Hill had left out a few minutes prior as they were in a hurry to board their private jet and get back to Dallas with the rest of their team.

Prinny saw their Uber pulling off as she and the girls were walking out to the hospital parking lot.

The eight women and their three cameramen were approaching their ride—a two-million-dollar Newell tour bus with an image of the full cast of *The Real Baddies of Chicago* plastered on the sides—when a blacked-out Mercedes Benz SUV whipped up behind them. The four burly bodyguards who'd accompanied the girls into, and out of, the hospital were fifteen paces behind; they lengthened their strides, but not by much for they knew what Princess knew—and what the other girls didn't.

Princess smiled widely.

"Who the hell is that?" Bunny XXX asked no one in general.

The rear driver's side door came open just a crack and Mike positioned his camera for the perfect shot.

"Ladies," Princess said. "I'd like to introduce you all to the newest member of *The Real Baddies* family."

The door swung all the way open then, and the girl leapt out to a chorus of unwelcoming groans and muttered expletives.

"Blicky Nicky!" Princess finished.

Season Three, Coming Soon…

Lock Down Publications and Ca$h Presents
Assisted Publishing Packages

Due to an increase in the price of services we have increased our prices. The prices below reflect the price increase as of 11/1/24.

BASIC PACKAGE $699 Editing Cover Design Formatting	UPGRADED PACKAGE $1000 Typing Editing Cover Design Formatting Upload eBooks to Amazon Upload Paperback to Amazon
ADVANCE PACKAGE $1,400 Typing Editing (line editing/content) Cover Design Formatting Copyright Registration Proofreading Upload eBooks to Amazon Upload Paperback to Amazon	LDP SUPREME PACKAGE $1,700 Typing Editing (line editing/content) Cover Design Formatting Copyright Registration Proofreading Set up Amazon Account Upload eBooks to Amazon Upload Paperback to Amazon Advertise on LDP's Amazon and Facebook Page

***
Other services available upon request.
Additional charges may apply

Lock Down Publications
P.O. Box 944
Stockbridge, GA 30281-9998
Phone: 470 303-9761
Email: lockdownpublications@gmail.com

Submission Guideline

Submit the first three chapters of your completed manuscript to ldpsubmissions@gmail.com. In the subject line add **Your Book's Title**. The manuscript must be in a Word Doc file and sent as an attachment. Document should be in Times New Roman, double spaced, and in size 12 font. Also, provide your synopsis and full contact information. If sending multiple submissions, they must each be in a separate email.

Have a story but no way to send it electronically? You can still submit to LDP/Ca$h Presents. Send in the first three chapters, written or typed, of your completed manuscript to:

LDP: Submissions Dept
P.O. Box 944
Stockbridge, GA 30281-9998

DO NOT send original manuscript. Must be a duplicate. Provide your synopsis and a cover letter containing your full contact information.

Thanks for considering LDP and Ca$h Presents.

NEW RELEASES

BLOODLINE OF A SAVAGE 1-3
THESE VICIOUS STREETS 1-3
RELENTLESS GOON 1-3
BY PRINCE A. TAUHID

THE BUTTERFLY MAFIA 1-3
BY FUMIYA PAYNE

A THUG'S STREET PRINCESS 1&2
BY MEESHA

CITY OF SMOKE 3
BY MOLOTTI

GET IT IN SLUGS 1 &2
BY B. STALL

STANDING ON HER BUSINESS 1&2
BY DG SANTANA

STEPPERS 1,2&3
THE REAL BADDIES OF CHI-RAQ
BY KING RIO

THE LANE 1&2
BY KEN-KEN SPENCE

THUG OF SPADES 1&2
LOVE IN THE TRENCHES 2
CORNER BOYS
BY COREY ROBINSON

TIL DEATH 3
BY ARYANNA

THE BIRTH OF A GANGSTER 4
BY DELMONT PLAYER

PRODUCT OF THE STREETS 1-3
BY DEMOND "MONEY" ANDERSON

NO TIME FOR ERROR
BY KEESE

MONEY HUNGRY DEMONS 1-2
BY TRANAY ADAMS

HUB CITY MENACE 1-3
BY J. WHITE

A THUGGISH PASSION 1&2
LAND OF DA HOOLIGANZ 1-4
KILLAZ ON STANDBY 1&2
BY IRA B.

FO'EVA ROLLIN 1&2
BY ASSA RAYMOND BAKER

THE LEVEL UP 1&3
BY LUXURY KING

Coming Soon from Lock Down Publications/Ca$h Presents

IF YOU CROSS ME ONCE 6
ANGEL V
By Anthony Fields

A THUGS STREET PRINCESS 3
By Meesha

CORNER BOYS 2
By Corey Robinson

THA TAKEOVER
By Keith Chandler

BETRAYAL OF A G 2
By Ray Vinci

SAVAGE FAMILY EMPIRE 1&2
SOULLESS GOON 1,2&3
THE DIRTY SIDE OF MONEY 1,2&3
By Prince

FOR MY ENEMY'S SAKE
AMBITIONS OF A SLIDER
FRESH OFF DA PORCH
By IRA B.

THE TRUCKLOAD 1-4
TIPPIN' THE SCALES 1-3
BAD BITCHES WIT GUNZ 3
PROBLEM SOLVED 2
By Christopher "Diesel" Hornezes

Available Now

RESTRAINING ORDER 1 & 2
By **CA$H & Coffee**

LOVE KNOWS NO BOUNDARIES 1-3
By **Coffee**

RAISED AS A GOON I, II, III & IV
BRED BY THE SLUMS I, II, III
BLAST FOR ME I & II
ROTTEN TO THE CORE I II III
A BRONX TALE I, II, III
DUFFLE BAG CARTEL I II III IV V VI
HEARTLESS GOON I II III IV V
A SAVAGE DOPEBOY I II
DRUG LORDS I II III
CUTTHROAT MAFIA I II
KING OF THE TRENCHES
By **Ghost**

LAY IT DOWN I & II
LAST OF A DYING BREED I II
BLOOD STAINS OF A SHOTTA I & II III
By **Jamaica**

LOYAL TO THE GAME I II III
LIFE OF SIN I, II III
By **TJ & Jelissa**

IF LOVING HIM IS WRONG…I & II
LOVE ME EVEN WHEN IT HURTS I II III
By **Jelissa**

PUSH IT TO THE LIMIT
By **Bre' Hayes**

BLOODY COMMAS I & II
SKI MASK CARTEL I, II & III
KING OF NEW YORK I II, III IV V
RISE TO POWER I II III
COKE KINGS I II III IV V
BORN HEARTLESS I II III IV
KING OF THE TRAP I II
By **T.J. Edwards**

WHEN THE STREETS CLAP BACK I & II III
THE HEART OF A SAVAGE I II III IV
MONEY MAFIA I II
LOYAL TO THE SOIL I II III
By **Jibril Williams**

A DISTINGUISHED THUG STOLE MY HEART I II & III
LOVE SHOULDN'T HURT I II III IV
RENEGADE BOYS 1-4
PAID IN KARMA 1-3
SAVAGE STORMS 1-3
AN UNFORESEEN LOVE 1-3
BABY, I'M WINTERTIME COLD 1-3
A THUG'S STREET PRINCESS 1&2
By **Meesha**

A GANGSTER'S CODE 1-3
A GANGSTER'S SYN 1-3
THE SAVAGE LIFE 1-3
CHAINED TO THE STREETS 1-3
BLOOD ON THE MONEY 1-3
A GANGSTA'S PAIN 1-3
BEAUTIFUL LIES AND UGLY TRUTHS
CHURCH IN THESE STREETS
By **J-Blunt**

CUM FOR ME 1-8
An LDP Erotica Collaboration

BLOOD OF A BOSS 1-5
SHADOWS OF THE GAME
TRAP BASTARD
By **Askari**

THE STREETS BLEED MURDER 1-3
THE HEART OF A GANGSTA 1-3
By **Jerry Jackson**

WHEN A GOOD GIRL GOES BAD
By **Adrienne**

THE COST OF LOYALTY 1-3
By **Kweli**

BRIDE OF A HUSTLA 1-3
THE FETTI GIRLS 1-3
CORRUPTED BY A GANGSTA 1-4
BLINDED BY HIS LOVE
THE PRICE YOU PAY FOR LOVE 1-3
DOPE GIRL MAGIC 1-3
By **Destiny Skai**

A KINGPIN'S AMBITION
A KINGPIN'S AMBITION II
I MURDER FOR THE DOUGH
By **Ambitious**

TRUE SAVAGE 1-7
DOPE BOY MAGIC 1-3
MIDNIGHT CARTEL 1-3
CITY OF KINGZ 1&2
NIGHTMARE ON SILENT AVE
THE PLUG OF LIL MEXICO 1&2
CLASSIC CITY
By **Chris Green**

A GANGSTER'S REVENGE 1-4
THE BOSS MAN'S DAUGHTERS 1-5
A SAVAGE LOVE 1&2
BAE BELONGS TO ME 1&2
A HUSTLER'S DECEIT 1-3
WHAT BAD BITCHES DO 1-3
SOUL OF A MONSTER 1-3
KILL ZONE
A DOPE BOY'S QUEEN 1-3
TIL DEATH 1-3
IMMA DIE BOUT MINE 1-6
DYING FOR LIKES
By **Aryanna**

A DOPEBOY'S PRAYER
By **Eddie "Wolf" Lee**

THE KING CARTEL 1-3
By **Frank Gresham**

THESE NIGGAS AIN'T LOYAL 1-3
By **Nikki Tee**

GANGSTA SHYT 1-3
By **CATO**

THE ULTIMATE BETRAYAL
By **Phoenix**

BOSS'N UP 1-3
By **Royal Nicole**

I LOVE YOU TO DEATH
By **Destiny J**

I RIDE FOR MY HITTA
I STILL RIDE FOR MY HITTA
By **Misty Holt**

LOVE & CHASIN' PAPER
By **Qay Crockett**

TO DIE IN VAIN
SINS OF A HUSTLA
By **ASAD**

BROOKLYN HUSTLAZ
By **Boogsy Morina**

BROOKLYN ON LOCK 1 & 2
By **Sonovia**

GANGSTA CITY
By **Teddy Duke**

A DRUG KING AND HIS DIAMOND 1-3
A DOPEMAN'S RICHES
HER MAN, MINE'S TOO 1&2
CASH MONEY HO'S
THE WIFEY I USED TO BE 1&2
PRETTY GIRLS DO NASTY THINGS
By **Nicole Goosby**

LIPSTICK KILLAH 1-3
CRIME OF PASSION 1-3
FRIEND OR FOE 1-3
By **Mimi**

TRAPHOUSE KING 1-3
KINGPIN KILLAZ 1-3
STREET KINGS 1&2
PAID IN BLOOD 1&2
CARTEL KILLAZ 1-3
DOPE GODS 1&2
By **Hood Rich**

THE STREETS ARE CALLING
By **Duquie Wilson**

STEADY MOBBN' 1-3
THE STREETS STAINED MY SOUL 1-3
By **Marcellus Allen**

WHO SHOT YA 1-3
SON OF A DOPE FIEND 1-4
HEAVEN GOT A GHETTO 1&2
SKI MASK MONEY 1&2
By **Renta**

GORILLAZ IN THE BAY 1-4
TEARS OF A GANGSTA 1/&2
3X KRAZY 1&2
STRAIGHT BEAST MODE 1&2
By **DE'KARI**

TRIGGADALE 1-3
MURDA WAS THE CASE 1-3
By **Elijah R. Freeman**

SLAUGHTER GANG 1-3
RUTHLESS HEART 1-3
By **Willie Slaughter**

GOD BLESS THE TRAPPERS 1-3
THESE SCANDALOUS STREETS 1-3
FEAR MY GANGSTA 1-5
THESE STREETS DON'T LOVE NOBODY 1-2
BURY ME A G 1-5
A GANGSTA'S EMPIRE 1-4
THE DOPEMAN'S BODYGAURD 1&2
THE REALEST KILLAZ 1-3
THE LAST OF THE OGS 1-3
By **Tranay Adams**

MARRIED TO A BOSS 1-3
By **Destiny Skai & Chris Green**

KINGZ OF THE GAME 1-7
CRIME BOSS 1-4
By **Playa Ray**

FUK SHYT
By **Blakk Diamond**

DON'T F#CK WITH MY HEART 1&2
By **Linnea**

ADDICTED TO THE DRAMA 1-3
IN THE ARM OF HIS BOSS
By **Jamila**

LOYALTY AIN'T PROMISED 1&2
By **Keith Williams**

YAYO 1-4
A SHOOTER'S AMBITION 1&2
BRED IN THE GAME
By **S. Allen**

TRAP GOD 1-3
RICH $AVAGE 1-3
MONEY IN THE GRAVE 1-3
CARTEL MONEY 1&2
By **Martell Troublesome Bolden**

FOREVER GANGSTA 1&2
GLOCKS ON SATIN SHEETS 1&2
By **Adrian Dulan**

TOE TAGZ 1-4
LEVELS TO THIS SHYT 1&2
IT'S JUST ME AND YOU
By **Ah'Million**

KINGPIN DREAMS 1-3
RAN OFF ON DA PLUG
By **Paper Boi Rari**

THE STREETS MADE ME 1-3
By **Larry D. Wright**

CONFESSIONS OF A GANGSTA 1-4
CONFESSIONS OF A JACKBOY 1-3
CONFESSIONS OF A HITMAN
CONFESSIONS OF A DOPE BOY
By **Nicholas Lock**

I'M NOTHING WITHOUT HIS LOVE
SINS OF A THUG
TO THE THUG I LOVED BEFORE
A GANGSTA SAVED XMAS
IN A HUSTLER I TRUST
By **Monet Dragun**

QUIET MONEY 1-3
THUG LIFE 1-3
EXTENDED CLIP 1&2
A GANGSTA'S PARADISE
By **Trai'Quan**

CAUGHT UP IN THE LIFE 1-3
THE STREETS NEVER LET GO 1-3
By **Robert Baptiste**

NEW TO THE GAME 1-3
MONEY, MURDER & MEMORIES 1-3
By **Malik D. Rice**

CREAM 2-3
THE STREETS WILL TALK
By **Yolanda Moore**

THE STREETS WILL NEVER CLOSE 1-3
By **K'ajji**

LIFE OF A SAVAGE 1-4
A GANGSTA'S QUR'AN 1-4
MURDA SEASON 1-3
GANGLAND CARTEL 1-3
CHI'RAQ GANGSTAS 1-4
KILLERS ON ELM STREET 1-3
JACK BOYZ N DA BRONX 1-3
A DOPEBOY'S DREAM 1-3
JACK BOYS VS DOPE BOYS 1-3
COKE GIRLZ
COKE BOYS
SOSA GANG 1&2
BRONX SAVAGES
BODYMORE KINGPINS
BLOOD OF A GOON
By **Romell Tukes**

CONCRETE KILLA 1-3
VICIOUS LOYALTY 1-3
BLOODY MONEY BAGS
By **Kingpen**

THE ULTIMATE SACRIFICE 1-6
KHADIFI
IF YOU CROSS ME ONCE 1-3
ANGEL 1-4
IN THE BLINK OF AN EYE
By **Anthony Fields**

THE LIFE OF A HOOD STAR
By **Ca$h & Rashia Wilson**

NIGHTMARES OF A HUSTLA 1-3
BLOOD AND GAMES 1&2
By **King Dream**

GHOST MOB
By **Stilloan Robinson**

HARD AND RUTHLESS 1&2
MOB TOWN 251
THE BILLIONAIRE BENTLEYS 1-3
REAL G'S MOVE IN SILENCE
By **Von Diesel**

MOB TIES 1-7
SOUL OF A HUSTLER, HEART OF A KILLER 1-3
GORILLAZ IN THE TRENCHES
OOPS CRY TOO 1&2
THE DAUGHTER OF A CARTEL BOSS
By **SayNoMore**

BODYMORE MURDERLAND 1-3
THE BIRTH OF A GANGSTER 1-4
By **Delmont Player**

FOR THE LOVE OF A BOSS 1&2
By **C. D. Blue**

KILLA KOUNTY 1-5
TENDER
By **Khufu**

MOBBED UP 1-4
THE BRICK MAN 1-5
THE COCAINE PRINCESS 1-10
STEPPERS 1-3
SUPER GREMLIN 1-4
A GANGSTA'S SON
By **King Rio**

MONEY GAME 1&2
By **Smoove Dolla**

A GANGSTA'S KARMA 1-5
By **FLAME**

KING OF THE TRENCHES 1-3
By **GHOST & TRANAY ADAMS**

BAD BITCHES WIT GUNZ 1&2
PROBLEM SOLVED
By "Christopher Diesel" Hornezes

QUEEN OF THE ZOO 1&2
By **Black Migo**

GRIMEY WAYS 1-3
BETRAYAL OF A G
By **Ray Vinci**

XMAS WITH AN ATL SHOOTER
By **Ca$h & Destiny Skai**

KING KILLA 1&2
By **Vincent "Vitto" Holloway**

BETRAYAL OF A THUG 1&2
By **Fre$h**

COUNTDOWN OF A KILLA 1&2
SEX, MURDER AND GOD 1&2
GUNS DOWN, BOTTOMS UP 1&2
By Lo-Life

THE MURDER QUEENS 1-7
By **Michael Gallon**

FOR THE LOVE OF BLOOD 1-4
By **Jamel Mitchell**

THE REAL BADDIES OF CHI-RAQ 2 | KING RIO

HOOD CONSIGLIERE 1&2
NO TIME FOR ERROR
By **Keese**

PROTÉGÉ OF A LEGEND 1,2&3
LOVE IN THE TRENCHES 1&2
By **Corey Robinson**

THE PLUG'S RUTHLESS DAUGHTER 1&2
By **Tony Daniels**

BORN IN THE GRAVE 1-3
CRIME PAYS
By **Self Made Tay**

MOAN IN MY MOUTH
By **XTASY**

TORN BETWEEN A GANGSTER AND A GENTLEMAN
By **J-BLUNT & Miss Kim**

LOYALTY IS EVERYTHING 1-3
CITY OF SMOKE 1-3
By **Molotti**

HERE TODAY GONE TOMORROW 1&2
By **Fly Rock**

WOMEN LIE MEN LIE 1-4
FIFTY SHADES OF SNOW 1-3
STACK BEFORE YOU SPLURGE
GIRLS FALL LIKE DOMINOES
NAÏVE TO THE STREETS
By **ROY MILLIGAN**

PILLOW PRINCESS
By **S. Hawkins**

THE REAL BADDIES OF CHI-RAQ 2 | KING RIO

THE BUTTERFLY MAFIA 1-3
SALUTE MY SAVAGERY 1&2
By **Fumiya Payne**

THE LANE 1&2
By Ken-Ken Spence

THE PUSSY TRAP 1-5
By **Nene Capri**

DIRTY DNA
By **Blaque**

SANCTIFIED AND HORNY
by **XTASY**

BOOKS BY LDP'S CEO, CA$H

TRUST IN NO MAN
TRUST IN NO MAN 2
TRUST IN NO MAN 3
BONDED BY BLOOD
SHORTY GOT A THUG
THUGS CRY
THUGS CRY 2
THUGS CRY 3
TRUST NO BITCH
TRUST NO BITCH 2
TRUST NO BITCH 3
TIL MY CASKET DROPS
RESTRAINING ORDER
RESTRAINING ORDER 2
IN LOVE WITH A CONVICT
LIFE OF A HOOD STAR
XMAS WITH AN ATL SHOOTER